Gracier

Milissa R. Bailey

Published by Boone River Publishing, LLC

Boone River Publishing, LLC
833 Walnut Street
Webster City IA 50595

Cover photography © Lane Lambert from iStockphoto

First Boone River Publishing, LLC edition May 2012

Boone River Publishing, LLC and colophon are registered trademarks.

For information about special discounts for bulk purchases, to schedule an event with the author or other inquiries, please email info@milissarbailey.com.

Manufactured in the United States of America

10 9 8 7 6 5 4 3 2 1

Library of Congress Control Number: 2012901369

ISBN 978-0-9850736-0-2
ISBN 978-0-9850736-1-9 (ebook)

For My Family,
My Parents who taught me to believe
My Children who remind me what is important
And My Husband who inspires me daily
Faith, Always

CHAPTER 1

The priest stood at the head of the coffin, a tattered black book in hand, his thumb rubbing the cover. It was obviously worn smooth from many days like this. The mourners filed under the small green canvas tent covering the ground next to Jonas McCabe's plot.

It was raining, a soft rain, one that floats down in misty blankets, clinging to all that is earthbound, condensing into little rivers.

She noticed the mist forming on the tops of her once glossy, now blurred patent leather heels had turned the dried Iowa dirt into what appeared to be little crumbs of moist chocolate cake. The dry grass under the awning reached up to brush the mud from her heels. Iowa soil was too thick and clung too tightly to be wiped clean by a fragile blade of grass.

Bodies pressed against each other behind her. Stepping forward she sat in the chair, the solitary chair. Being an only child followed you everywhere.

The chanting began and the awning muffled voices

hushed in respect.

Holding the long chains of the incense-filled chalice in one hand and swinging it with the other, Father Patrick circled the oak coffin.

The "chinging" of the chains on the container's shining gold exterior was one of the sounds of death. To Jessica it brought to mind the final scene from "It's a Wonderful Life" ...*another angel getting his wings.*

Her eyes came to the top of the long oak expanse. Strange, such beautiful flowers lain on top of a coffin so dark and sad.

The chanting stopped. Father Patrick mumbled the final words of the traditional Catholic funeral and made the sign of the cross over the box that contained her grandfather.

He walked to her, the last of the McCabes. "Jessica, God's peace be with you." He squeezed her hand.

Moving out from under the tent, his robes fluttering in the wind, the priest proceeded up the hill, the young altar boy following him.

Her adopted uncle, the gentlest of souls, came forward, shared an embrace, then left as if he knew she needed these last moments alone.

Little by little, the crowd dwindled until nothing lingered but the silence and Jessica McCabe.

Jessica stepped to the coffin. The rain fell, and as the water cascaded, she could feel the few loose strands that framed her cheeks curling into perfect ringlets.

The sky's tears mixed with hers. She turned her face upward asking the gray weeping clouds to wash away the pain. They continued to cry together...alone.

She stood in the mist not concerned with the dampness that engulfed her. Jessica touched the coffin and allowed the sadness to seep in, her guard down. Something she rarely did. But she was so tired. The long suppressed anguish racked her body.

"Jess."

The deep baritone penetrated the sorrow in which she had cloaked herself. Jessica inhaled slowly, drawing in all that she had let go of. Rigid, she turned.

He ran his tan fingers through his wavy black hair. A nervous habit he hadn't outgrown. Surrounded in shadows, there was still sufficient light to catch the emotion that glistened in his deep, emerald green eyes. *This is not the time or place to deal with this, with him. There never would be.*

He came forward, leaving the corner of the tent. She could sense his apprehension.

Even now. *Here.* The same effect. She hated it with every fiber of her being. His familiar scent invaded and sent her reeling...this was all too much.

"Jess." He touched her.

It was still there, the intensity, years of denial, gone.

Without warning, Jessica's head was on his broad chest, unleashed sorrow staining his shirt and tie. His arms went around her and although tarnished by the moment, she sank into the support of his body.

He didn't move, his response, a shock of cold water. *He is his father's son. How had she loved such a man?* The fresh pain fulfilled its purpose. Her resolve strengthened.

Jessica withdrew, abandoning the arms that had briefly shut out the world, embarrassed at the loss of self-control.

She pulled a small white tissue from her purse. A purse. She could count on one hand the number of times she had carried one. The whole day had been an out-of-sort puzzle, this, just another piece.

"I'm sorry...I'm not quite...I'm..." *Damn.* The only person she hated more than him right now was herself.

Taking a deep breath, she lifted her eyes, drawing slowly upward until she looked into Matthew Cassidy's suntanned face. "It's nice of you to come, Matthew. Although, Jonas is giving you hell right now for wasting your time. You know what he..." She decided to take the high road. "What he thought of funerals."

"He's probably giving us both a piece of his mind right now."

The comment's double meaning required no explanation.

He drew somber. His intense gaze hinted at something she refused to acknowledge.

His hand finding hers again, he gently nestled it. "Jess, I'm so sorry about Jonas."

Defiant at Matthew's attempt to regain the moment, she withdrew.

He awkwardly placed his hand in his suit pants pocket.

"Well..." Jess motioned to the limousine. Tired, overwhelmed, she grasped desperately at the emotions fighting to escape.

She approached the casket and drew a single yellow rose from the cascading blooms. Finished, Jessica started up the hill to the car.

Matthew took her elbow. She did not withdraw, appreciating the kind steadiness he offered.

The funeral director, Mr. O'Connor, opened the car door.

"Will you take over the practice?" Matthew's voice was but a whisper, nervous.

"Honestly, I haven't thought any further than today." She got into the car. *Keep it together.* "Thank you for coming, Matthew. Ready Mr. O'Connor."

Jessica tucked the wandering strands of damp hair into place. She ran her hand across the fabric of the simple black dress. *Lord, am I ready to be out of this.*

She fought the desire to look. *Is he still there?*

Her mind's floodgates opened. The turbulent waters of what they had been swirled. She did not have the strength or energy for this, not now, not ever.

Jessica set her thoughts to the day's next event - dinner in the church hall served by the funeral committee, as with all funerals in this small Midwestern town a tradition.

Oh Lord, let Steven be there. Best friends since second grade, she hadn't seen him all day. *Where could he be?*

Jessica looked out the tinted window as the car navigated the cemetery's circular drive to the McCabe family plot. The loneliness she'd been trying to avoid all day wrapped around her.

"Mr. O'Connor, stop the car please."

The funeral home director slowed the car as she tried to take it in.

The headstones stood on the freshly mowed grounds, a final calling card to those who passed.

JONAS MCCABE
BORN NOVEMBER 28, 1912.

Her grandfather's had always been there, the date of death absent.

ANN MCCABE
BORN JUNE 10, 1913
DIED JULY 1963.

North of the two black granite headstones laid a small rose-colored one. It bore the name of a woman Jessica had merely known from a handful of pictures and a heartbroken father's memories.

Jonas had told the story on two occasions. It had been difficult for him to discuss. However, he understood the little girl and the young woman who had asked him to explain the circumstances of her mother's premature death sought answers. Not only for peace of mind, but moreover, to have something to hold on to, even the briefest of memories.

Jessica recalled her seventh birthday. Jonas had thrown a party and invited her entire class, including a child new to the class who asked where Jessica's mother was.

A classmate's whisper had resonated all too loudly, "She has no mother, she's an orphan."

Jessica pretended not to hear, but she couldn't hide the

hurt.

The party over, presents piled high, Jessica's grandfather lifted the little girl he had raised on to his lap.

She could hear his voice and the sadness.

"It was love at first sight." He winked. *"When they finally let her hold you, she sang you to sleep with an Irish lullaby..."* he faltered. *"The one your grandmother used to sing.*

"She asked me to hold you. She was tired." Tears sparkled, shining with a love she knew as limitless. *"I wanted to be mad at God for taking Maggie. But this,"* he cupped her face in his calloused hand, *"this wouldn't let me."*

Jessica wiped his cheeks.

"God got his angel. And I got mine."

Jessica's mother had suffered unexpected complications.

Jonas McCabe, in one brief moment, lost his only child and became his granddaughter's only hope.

MARGARET MARIE MCCABE
IN GOD'S LOVING CARE
SPRING 1963

Jessica stared at the pale pink headstone.

SPRING 1963

The one thing Jonas had permitted in the way of dating

his daughter's death.

The rivers of mist on the tinted car windows became more and more frequent. Jessica drew her gaze within the car. Mr. O'Connor pulled away.

The line of cars paraded in a solemn procession, each taking its own path once at the cemetery gates.

She wanted to be anywhere but in this place.

"If you prefer, I can drive you to the church? Someone can wait there to give you a ride to your car at the funeral home."

Jessica met his concerned expression.

He turned in the direction of St. John's Catholic Church.

Not much had changed in this "Norman Rockwell" like community where she'd grown up. She seldom came into town on visits home. She had preferred to stay out on the farm with Jonas.

The houses of Gracier, Iowa remained basically the same today as they were fifty years ago, except for a half dozen coats of paint and a new shrub or tree here and there.

Mixed among them were those unmistakable homes of an old school Catholic, easily recognized by the statue of the Virgin Mary on display. The statues set in white alcoves, which in many cases consisted of a cast iron bathtub painted white stood on end submerged halfway into the owner's yard, enshrining the holiest Mother of the church.

Jessica had cherished this town growing up. The fact she was the daughter of an unwed mother and the gossip that resulted had had little effect. She had three men to thank for that. Their mission in life to ensure she was surrounded by people who loved and cared for her.

In front of St. John's Catholic Church, Mr. O'Connor stepped out. She recognized the look, pity for the wagging tongues she was about to encounter.

Thirty years, the same gossip, nonetheless some people couldn't hold their tongues. And the "windiest" windbag, none other than the funeral home director's wife.

Funny, she felt as much pity for him. True, she would have to tolerate the gossiping busy body, but he had to live with her.

"The sun may pop out later." He glanced at the sky gradually getting lighter. "But just in case, take this."

Jessica accepted the umbrella.

She was aware of him watching her. The dread rose to the surface again.

"Don't worry, Jessica." His hand rested tenderly on her shoulder.

She advanced up the wide cement sidewalk to the church hall.

Several years had come and gone since she'd entered St. John's. She'd come then to find hope and answers. No comfort, only sorrow had followed. More than God had abandoned Jessica that day.

"Let's get it over with then." She reached for the well-worn brass handle polished to a shine from the many that had grasped it.

Mr. O'Connor held the heavy oak door for Jessica.

The "Church Ladies" as Jessica referred to them welcomed her. A mainstay of virtually every parish, a group of women, there no matter the event... wedding, funeral or anniversary, working with an urgency that would put the U.S. Army to shame.

And the St. John "Church Ladies" took great pride in typifying the vocation. Maids in waiting, they hovered over her. Ushered to the head table, a hot plate of scalloped potatoes and ham, coffee and milk awaited.

The mourners, chattering among themselves, paused momentarily upon Jessica's entrance.

Father Patrick appeared snacking on a piping hot roll. Wiping his hands, he brushed the evidence of his indulgence onto the church hall's tile floor.

He was Friar Tuck incarnate. Thinning ring of brown hair circling the bald crown of his head, round weeble shaped body and the jolliest of fellows. But the humble disposition could be deceiving, as Jonas McCabe had found him a more than worthy opponent during weekly Sunday afternoon chess games.

He had come to the parish when Jessica was eleven, and upon retiring, had decided to live in the area, filling in when called upon. A family friend, Jessica had asked him to preside at Jonas' funeral mass.

He'd met Jessica at the farm upon her arrival home. Offering his sympathies, he had then helped himself to a cookie from the perpetually full cookie jar. They had discussed the burial mass and other matters.

Jonas had made it a point to attend wakes and funerals of Gracier's citizens, whether passing acquaintances or friends.

That along with being the local veterinarian for fifty plus

years, she and Father Patrick had fully expected his funeral would be a large affair.

He would have hated all this. Jonas had never liked "big to-do's" over anything he did, and certainly not passing on.

"Let us pray."

The drone quieted and heads bowed in reverence.

Steven, where are you? Jessica scanned the crowd, their eyes cast down in prayer. *World traveler that he is, maybe he hadn't heard. No, his mother must have gotten a hold of him by now.*

Her closest confidant, they had shared each other's hopes, dreams and tragedies. As the demands of their careers had separated them, it hadn't severed the bond.

They'd talked a week ago. He was leaving to cover the latest political campaign for *Viewpoint*, the magazine he'd worked at since graduating.

He'd called out of the blue to see how she was doing. Funny, had the call been a couple hours later--

"Amen." Father Patrick lowered his arms and addressed those gathered around him. "There's plenty to eat, we'll begin the line with this table." He pointed a finger to the south end of the hall. "The ladies prepared a fine meal." He patted his round stomach, and the mourners chuckled at his good-natured humor.

Already served, Jessica nibbled at the generous helpings. It was only out of consideration to the ladies that she attempted to eat.

As friends, community leaders, and farmers filed by, Jessica listened politely to the casual chatter. Some stopped for a brief moment, while others moved forward in the line, cordial and silent.

Chester Caughlin, one of her two adopted uncles, sat next to her at the table, conversing with those paying their respects.

Jessica had been brought up under the watchful eyes of two other men besides Jonas, "The Three Musketeers". They were a part of her earliest memories.

As she thought back over the last few days, Jessica realized she'd been selfish. The support, the resolute strength, what would she have done without them?

While she had lost a grandfather, they had lost a brother, if not by blood, more surely by love. The third in this band of merry men, however, was not present, and he was the one she was most worried about.

She put her hand on Chester's. "You look so tired."

A leathery landscape, Chester Caughlin's worn features told of a hardworking, often burden-filled life. His ruddy cheeks contrasted drastically with his stark white forehead, the signature look of an Iowa farmer. But in his case, it was due to his many years as the County Sheriff.

"I'm fine." He grasped Jessica's hand. "You're the one who needs rest, child. People would well understand. Go home to the farm. I'll come out and check on you later."

"Not a chance." Jessica leaned and whispered into his good ear. "Besides, if I left you alone, who knows what Miss Pickering might have in mind?"

Chester Caughlin frowned half-heartedly.

Since Chester's wife had passed on, Miss Pickering had

set her sights on this eligible widower. He had played it to be an irritation. She suspected the retired sheriff had begun to enjoy the attention.

Jess winked. "You belong to me."

The old man's crooked grin showed how important this designation was to him.

The two fell silent. The void filled with the church hall's hum of activity. Gradually the voices locked in idle conversation lulled and the gathering began to thin.

Crossing the room to the kitchen, Jessica was stopped at almost every table by people reminding her to not be afraid to ask for help. *Iowa hospitality*.

Then, she saw Joseph Cassidy. His presence, not a shock, the lack of a production, until now, was.

He walked from the far end of the church hall, his attention riveted on the last McCabe.

Jessica had always been uneasy around him, and it had intensified.

Joseph Cassidy had practiced law in Gracier for twenty years, and considered himself a fourth generation farmer. The manicured nails and smooth hands accented by mother of pearl cuff links at each wrist did not exhibit the labor his ancestors had experienced.

"Jessica, please accept my condolences." He extended his right hand.

She did not hesitate to meet the arrogance head on. This man held a unique distinction, the one person Jonas McCabe had truly disliked. He had never shared the details behind the contention. Jessica had a pretty good idea though, land was at the heart of it. Regardless, the burning hatred had been apparent in any dealings that involved the longtime Gracier attorney.

"Joseph." She observed a faint scar on the inside of his thumb. Faded, it was his hand's only blemish. "I would tell you Jonas appreciates your respects, but why pretend."

Joseph appeared not to hear.

She felt confident he had.

The haunting resemblance to Maggie triggered the reaction once again. He maintained, detached, aloof. Joseph nodded a cordial greeting to Sheriff Caughlin and left.

***

The encounter over, Jessica pushed the swinging door into the kitchen. The ladies bustled quickly around Jessica's entrance.

Wise Miss Pickering pointed to the leftovers. "I'll have Chester drop a package by the farm later for you dear."

Jessica looked at the round little woman with plump powdered cheeks, precisely pressed apron and the strategic capability of a general. She would be a welcome member to Jessica's family.

Having finished one more round of the hall, she returned to where Chester stood visiting. The gathering dispersed.

"Mr. O'Connor said the car is outside for you. Let's go get your Jeep." Chester donned his Stetson.

Although she was quite capable, this was his way of helping as well as working through Jonas' death. Doting, always protecting. Today this solid steady man gave her upside down world a sense of balance.

"I'm okay, Chester. You stay and visit."

"Young lady--"

She hugged him, no chance to argue.

"Don't go doing any chores until I get there tomorrow to help, okay?"

Weaving her way to the church's side entry, anxious someone would intervene, Jessica held the door cautiously, until it closed with a muffled click.

The sun had come out, evaporating the rain's misty curtain and the wetness covering the day's early morning hours.

Jessica forgot about the ride Mr. O'Connor had promised and began walking to the funeral home eight blocks away.

The shoes she had worn were not meant for this excursion, causing her usual rapid stride to slow. It fit in well with the day's events, as everything had moved at this drawn out pace.

***

The sun glistened through the front windshield of his pickup. Matthew stared straight ahead unfazed by its intense brilliance. The cemetery empty now except for his truck.

He hadn't been prepared for how hard it would be. *Dear God, I can't do this. What if she stays?* His eyes drew skyward past the few remaining clouds that drifted in the now intense blue sky. *I kept my promise, old man. You better have kept yours.*

CHAPTER 2

It was unseasonably warm for October in Iowa. The smell of the wet fall foliage mixed with the earthy rich aroma of a newly plowed field filled Jessica's senses.

Coming to the corner, she stopped for a car, its driver paying little attention to the speed limit. Suddenly it slowed though there was no stop sign.

She couldn't see who was behind the wheel as the ascending noon sun bounced off the car's windshield.

Then Jessica saw the wave. *Steven!*

The car pulled to the curb, his long lanky arms were around her.

"Oh Jess." He turned her head toward him. "Mom didn't get a hold of me until late yesterday. I drove all night, but... ah damn, Jess."

Close to him again she was overwhelmed with relief.

Her tears subsided and she endeavored to steer the conversation away from her uncharacteristic behavior. "How goes the campaign coverage?" She noticed the shoulder of

Steven's jacket was wet and tried to wipe away the evidence.

"Not important. I just wish I hadn't been so damn far away. Leave it to your grandfather. His timing is usually better than this." He stopped, wincing.

"He probably did it just to tick you off." Jessica laughed. Steven knew better than to worry about offending her.

"Come on, let's go. People will wonder what in the world we're doing out here."

He led her to the passenger side of the red MG convertible. "At your service, Madam." Bending at the waist, his left arm swooped, slicing the air.

The unexpected "knight in shining armor" routine was just what she needed.

Steven stood erect again and shut the door behind her. Going around the rear of the car, he reached the driver's side and jumping, landed gingerly in the leather bucket seat.

"What was that, Sir Galahad?"

"Oh, M'lady," Steven seized Jessica's hand gallantly, "I am but here to serve your loveliness." He kissed it.

"Oh brother." Jessica rolled her eyes skyward.

Steven, cross-eyed, broke the spell of gallantry and the autumn air filled with laughter the two had shared since childhood.

"Well, Jess," Steven turned the ignition and the car revved to life again, "where are we headed?"

Jessica really hadn't thought much past getting to the farm. Now she wasn't so anxious to go home. She felt lost and confused. She didn't like it. Indecision had never been one of her weaknesses. Stubbornness, yes.

"Hungry?" Steven pointed in the direction of Gracier's tiny downtown. "It's a little past noon, but it shouldn't be too busy at Hannah's."

"I'm fine." She had no appetite. "You haven't had lunch yet have you?" Jessica spotted a parking space in front of the restaurant. "Let's pull in and you can grab a bite."

"Naaa." Steven cruised right on by the eating establishment. "I ate on the road."

Cars usually lined the street outside the diner at noontime. Today, most of Hannah's regulars had attended the funeral dinner instead.

On a normal day, farmers in for a break ate at Hannah's. In today's world of two family incomes, many farm wives worked outside the home. So Hannah's kept busy with those displaced fellows for many a meal.

Her grandfather had grown up on the very farm he'd lived on until his death. Many of his clients, who he considered friends, represented the third, fourth, even fifth generation to raise livestock on the same homestead.

So on his daily noon visit to Hannah's, Jonas chatted with the farmers on the latest happenings. It helped him to keep acquainted with his "patients" and in turn, farmers didn't need to take time out to call the local vet when a simple visit at lunch would do.

Jonas had loved being Gracier's veterinarian.

As a little girl, Jessica had tagged along on those trips to town. She wasn't sure which she had enjoyed more, the attention given to her by those weary fellows, even during the fall season when their energy was harvested into every bushel, or the delicious home cooked meals Hannah served.

The small cafe wasn't fancy by any means. Its walls covered with faded yellow wallpaper featured small light brown and orange caricatures of antique kitchen utensils, coffee pots, coffee mills, and hand held egg beaters.

Funny, those identical glorified kitchenwares were still put to use every day in the restaurant's tiny kitchen.

In the middle of the restaurant sat a U-shaped counter encircled by red vinyl stools attached to the floor.

Oh, to sit on those stools, spinning round and round until the kitchen utensils on the wallpaper and the figures seated around her became a blur.

Booths with alternating red and yellow vinyl seats lined the outside walls of the cafe. The tabletops in between were gray with red, yellow and silver specks. Metal bands surrounded the table edges, worn away until now only smooth silver strips resided where variegated ridges used to be.

Her grandfather's usual seat was the second booth in on the north wall flanking a large picture window. He never stated his reason for the specific seat, but she had a hunch. The booth offered a first-hand view of the front door and Gracier's Main Street.

Jessica wondered who would sit in the booth at lunchtime now. Shading her eyes against the noonday sun, she attempted to see into the diner's front window, but it was reflecting a bright blue autumn sky.

"What's wrong?" Steven tried to follow Jessica's line of sight.

"Just wondered who's up for lunch at Hannah's." She shifted forward again as they breezed through the narrow main street to the edge of town.

"How about a cruise to Kelly's Ridge? Bet it's pretty out there."

Jessica nodded at Steven's invitation, and he obliged by heading west on the road to the park.

Throughout high school and college, if either needed to think it was a given they could find their troubled friend at the Ridge looking out over the lazy, sometimes rushing river. They found solitude there.

Autumn leaves scurried, dodging the path of the red sports car traveling the tree-lined corridor hugging the river's edge. Gravel crunched and popped in its wake.

Jessica removed the scarf holding her hair. The breeze swept up the nape of her neck, lifting the soft curls and asking them to waltz.

The oak trees, solemn sentinels guarding the end of the season, towered overhead. Jessica focused on the unmatched natural beauty, desperate to push from her mind the week's events.

Steven slowed the car as they came upon the waterfall at the north end of the park. Not Niagara by any means, its cascading waters still caused a mist to ascend skyward. Meeting with the afternoon sun, the fine spray of water bloomed into tiny dancing rainbows and coaxed the fish into jumping for a glimpse at the world outside their watery globe.

The scene captured why Jessica found such peace here.

Steven stopped the car.

The ridge on the opposite shore shot up for a good 100 feet. The stone wall of a mighty fortress, walling out the world.

Jessica pulled her knees up to her chest, letting the dress fall, discreetly hiding her legs under its black folds.

"Were there a lot of people there today?"

Dear friend that he was, he knew she needed to talk.

"Matthew came." There, she'd said it and now awaited the consequences.

"Sure, like I don't feel bad enough." He clutched his chest grasping at an imaginary dagger. "Now you tell me I was upstaged by Sir Lancelot himself." His head fell as he gasped one last Shakespearean breath.

"He was nice Steven." Jessica wasn't going to let him get off that easy. "He didn't say a whole lot...I guess he--"

"You guess what?" Steven stared up into the never-ending blue above him. "That maybe he couldn't come up with anything cruel at the moment, or perhaps he's keeping up appearances, Dad is pretty prominent these days. Or maybe he thought this could be his penance!"

Jessica got out of the sports car and crossed the gravel to the well-worn picnic table. Sitting, she faced the water's edge.

Steven had reacted out of fierce loyalty for his self-proclaimed "little sister". He was the epitome of the overprotective brother, especially when it came to Matthew. She couldn't be angry with him.

The car door slammed. His conscience had given him a

good once over. Guilt got the better of him.

"I'm sorry." Beside her, Steven's long wiry frame draped the table. "It's just, after all he did and yet he acts as if nothing-—"

"You mean what his father did." Jessica argued. It was not only Steven she hoped to convince in the case of Matthew's innocence. "Matthew had nothing to do with--"

He sighed. His exasperation clear signaled the effort to hold his tongue. It was no use. "Spare me, Jess." There was no mistaking the hatred.

They'd had this discussion. He wanted Jessica to admit Matthew's involvement. She couldn't, not yet.

"His whole family would have benefited! Matthew admitted he knew about the foreclosures. Granted, the Cassidys didn't get their hands on the land, but those people had the property they'd owned for generations taken out from under them."

"It got stopped." Jessica interrupted Steven's lecture. "They don't own the land anymore, but they still get to farm it."

"Thanks to your grandfather and Doc Harrison." Steven footnoted. His lack of acceptance in regards to forgiveness for Matthew Cassidy or his family, blatant.

"And that's what I don't understand."

Steven's expression hid nothing. She had taken a sharp right, and he had no idea where she was headed.

"The money?" Jessica glanced at Steven. "Doc and he had money put away, but that's a lot of land for those two to buy. And cash rent can't nearly cover the debt. Especially the rate they probably gave those families."

"Did you ask about it?"

He'd dropped the Cassidy issue. Under different circumstances, Steven wouldn't have given in so easily. But he had, and she was grateful for him, her ever-faithful sounding board.

"I called home one night, pretty late." Jessica pondered over the events of the call. "The phone barely rang twice and he picked up. So I know he couldn't have been in bed. There's no way he could make it from his bedroom upstairs to the kitchen that fast." Jessica drew her brow tight.

"Jonas, up late?" Steven interrupted. "That isn't unusual Jess. He's done stranger things."

"That isn't it, Steven." Jessica shook her head. "There were voices in the background. I recognized Andrew's right away but there was at least one more. And when I asked him who was there so late at night, he told me Andrew, keeping him up with a game of Gin Rummy."

"Come on Jess, your grandfather, Gin Rummy. He used to keep us up until all hours playing cards."

"That's just it, Steven. Jonas loved cards...Doc loathed cards. They would sit on the porch Sunday afternoons arguing over which board game to play because Andrew refused to play cards."

"Well maybe Jonas won the argument."

"No...No, I heard another voice."

"Like some kind of conspiracy." He raised his eyebrows. "Maybe he had a lady friend, or maybe Chester had violated curfew?" Steven chuckled. "Theda kept a pretty short leash on him."

Jessica knew all too well the wrath of Chester's now deceased wife. "No. Jonas was acting... like I had caught him at something. I can't explain it."

Finding a twig on the table, she twirled it between her thumb and forefinger. "Anyway, a few days later he calls me one afternoon at the clinic and tells me what he and Doc are up to with the land deal. He asked if I had a problem if he mortgaged the farm. I told him I trusted whatever they decided to do."

"Your grandfather and the partners had a plan in the case of someone's death, right?...Jess?"

"*Steven*?" Jessica immersed herself in his gaze. There was no way he could bluff.

"You got me, Jess! I'm a miser by trade, and my hordes of cash from pilfering faraway lands more than helped pay off the debt owed." He finished, a cocked eyebrow confirming how ridiculous the insinuation was. "Where in the world would I get that kind of money, Jessica? I don't own anything worth mortgaging, and I'm not exactly thrifty." He directed her attention to the red sports car, his latest indulgence.

"Okay...okay, but there was someone else there." Jessica sighed in frustration.

"I understand Jonas and Doc were the main partners behind the Land Corporation, but did he ever tell you who the rest of the partners are?" Steven leaned on his elbows.

"No, just that he and Doc and a few other small investors paid off the land by mortgaging properties or with savings they had." She glimpsed at him. "According to Jonas and Doc, the other people involved demanded complete anonymity."

"That's not surprising, Jess. Folks around here don't take charity, and chances are if they discovered a neighbor had taken care of their debt, partnership or not, they'd have a tough time with it. But in Doc and Jonas' case, it was an investment."

Jessica nodded hesitantly in agreement. Something didn't ring true. "Well, shall we?" Standing up, she straightened her skirt, and walked to the car.

She appreciated the silence as they drove back through the park and into town.

***

Steven revved the motor. The red sports car's finely tuned engine echoed off the homes lining the street.

Flashes of auburn rode the wind beside him. *Did she know how beautiful, truly captivating she was?*

They'd been friends since second grade. He wouldn't trade that for a minute. However, he would give anything to find the courage to tell this woman the truth. The desire to be more than a "surrogate brother".

"Steven, God gave me the perfect family including the best big brother any sister could ever ask for!" And, as always, she ended her declaration with a kiss.

He wished he could have offered more than "brotherly" love.

Glancing briefly at the silhouette against the autumn sky, he ached to hold her in his arms. To share the passion withheld.

"Can you take me to Doc's?"

Barely audible above the sound of the motor, she startled him into the moment at hand.

He wasn't surprised by the request. He had no doubt Dr. Andrew Harrison needed to see Jessica too.

CHAPTER 3

Steven turned onto Maple Avenue towards the huge brick house at the end of the street. A home towering three stories above the earth, it contained 15 rooms not including the attic. A perfect medieval castle, it inspired the fantasies of Jessica's youth when kings and queens leapt from her imagination to create an afternoon of adventure.

When the nearest clinic had been fifty miles away, this enormous home with its dark weather worn bricks had served as office, clinic, and in many cases, hospital.

His home for over 50 years, Doc had kept the house even though technology had dictated it obsolete. He would be lost if he ever sold, having raised four children in the home with his wife, Ellie. Each had a family now and only came to visit on occasion.

Jessica hurt for how seldom Doc's children came to see him.

Like Chester, Doctor Andrew Harrison had been a big part of Jessica and Jonas' lives, their eclectic family.

And they had all shared in Doc's sadness when he lost Ellie to cancer 15 years ago.

Steven, steering up the driveway, went around to the rear of the house. People who knew Doc went to the back.

Jessica slipped on the black pumps and proceeded up the field stone steps. Taking the cast iron knocker in her hand, she tapped.

She could hear a shuffling noise. The dark walnut door opened to a man dressed in khaki pants, a plaid flannel shirt and navy sweater. He held a coffee mug and under his arm, a book.

Doctor Andrew Harrison looked drained. Like her, a toll taken.

Jessica had headed home the minute she got the call. Andrew and Chester had sat by Jonas' bedside for the short while he lived.

She was halfway home when she got the second call. Andrew had pronounced him dead at 10:05 AM.

Arriving about 30 minutes later, Chester was waiting. Andrew, after notifying the appropriate people, had gone. She assumed it had been too much.

"Jessica." Andrew swung the door wide. "And Steven, back with another adventure under your belt."

The turmoil eased.

Andrew held her tight.

The silence between filled with pain. She could feel his chest rise as he took a deep, steadying breath. Putting his arm around her, he escorted Jessica to the front parlor.

A large room filled with antiques and collectibles, all

polished to a shine. Doctor Andrew Harrison was a fanatic for cleanliness.

"Something to drink or eat?" Andrew looked first at Jessica then Steven.

"I'd take a cup of what you're having." Jessica acknowledged the mug on the coffee table in front of her.

Steven, sitting in the wingback chair to his right, nodded. "Sounds good."

Doc Andrew tilted his head. "Carlotta?"

The small round woman bustled into the room, dishtowel in hand. Her little wrinkled brown face lit up.

"Oh, my little Jesseeca," Carlotta's Mexican accent was still heavy.

She'd been with him since Ellie had become ill, taking care of the household duties as well as the doctor. He depended on Carlotta more then he would ever admit.

"Hello, Carlotta." Jessica's lungs fought for air as she received the signature Carlotta welcome, a full bear hug.

"My little Jessi." The compassionate hands that cradled Jessica's face hinted fresh baked cinnamon rolls and lemon. "Your poor little heart, it is so sad." Employer or not, they were all Carlotta's charges. Tenderness flowed, "It will heal...I promise you."

"Carlotta, these two need some tea." Andrew interrupted.

Carlotta's heart-rending reception tested Andrew's resolve. Always the caregiver.

"Would you please bring us a plate of cookies or whatever you've been banging around in there cooking this morning?"

Carlotta ignored her employer and smiled at Jessica. Then removing her hands, she turned to Steven, who towered above the short little Mexican woman.

"Carlotta!"

She feigned anger as her feet left the ground.

Planting a kiss on Carlotta's cheek, he placed her back on the floor.

"You!" Carlotta huffed, straightening her apron. "Flirting with a woman twice your age!"

Steven winked.

She spun on her heel, scurrying her stout little figure back to the kitchen. She tried to hide it, but Jessica spotted the joy his teasing gave Carlotta in the hallway mirror.

Andrew's red-rimmed eyes witnessed her amusement.

"Have you slept?"

"Young lady, I suspect you don't have much room to be asking such a question," he scolded. "May I ask when was the last--"

"No you may not."

Andrew turned the tables any time someone showed him compassion. A well-honed trait developed over decades of caring for others.

"You both look like hell," Steven broke the standoff.

"He's not slept since Jonas died." Carlotta, never afraid to speak her mind, had entered the room with a tray of tea and cookies. "He's going to get sick, and then you know who will be listening to his growling." She set the tray on the table.

Andrew glared as she poured more tea into his cup. "I'll be damned if you can find good help these days."

"Lucky for you, tiz not a problem." Carlotta left the room, strutting in a fashion that indicated to Jessica she was confident she'd won the round.

For a moment, there was silence.

"He didn't suffer, Jessica. It hit him so fast. He never came to again."

Jessica observed the old doctor as he placed his cup on the table. "Andrew, what was he doing out in the office so late at night? Especially if he wasn't feeling good?"

"With Jonas...well you know your grandfather."

She heard the hesitation. Grief? Or something he was afraid to tell her? *Trying to protect his little farm girl.* She held her tongue, he meant well.

But Jessica was far from satisfied. Jonas had not been himself lately, and she suspected Andrew had the answers.

"Andrew, where are the partnership papers?"

Dr. Harrison, holding the fresh pot of tea, filled the cups. "Cream, young man?"

Steven nodded as Andrew all too intently poured cream into each cup.

"Ever since the land deal..." Jessica leaned forward. "Was it the partnership?"

"How about you my dear, cream?"

Andrew, distant, strangely unconcerned, struck a chord.

"Is there a problem with it?" Jessica realized her accusing tone. "Please, Andrew, what would upset Jonas so much that it might induce a stroke?"

Andrew stirred the ivory colored liquid into his tea. "I don't believe any one thing caused his stroke."

The emotional dust settled around them.

"Were there a lot of people there today?" Andrew retrieved his pipe from the ashtray and lit it, puffing until white ribbons of smoke appeared.

The smell of sweet tobacco, Doc's smell, and to this day, if the air carried upon it the scent of a pipe, Jessica would turn half expecting to see him.

"The entire town, or close to it." Jessica sipped her tea. "Jonas would have hated it."

"I bet he gave Gabriel an earful today." Andrew chuckled. White tufts billowed, giving the appearance of a miniature steam engine.

Then, his tone changed, the words almost lost in the hovering pipe smoke. "The will is to be read on Tuesday. Jonas named you and me co-executors to his estate. I hope that's okay, Jessica?"

"I'm glad, Andrew." He must be hurting. The depth, no one would ever see. "I couldn't do this alone."

Andrew's eyes filled with tears. The all too familiar gaze rested on Jessica. The striking resemblance to her mother Maggie caused it more often than she could count. She supposed it should bother her.

Jessica set the teacup on the table and gently squeezed his hand. "I'm so thankful you were with him Andrew."

He was struggling to maintain. For Dr. Andrew Harrison a rare battle indeed. Known for his selfless bedside manner, it would be entirely out of character for him to seek comfort.

Andrew patted her hand, then got up.

Jessica and Steven stood to leave.

"Who will be there for the reading?"

"I'm not sure, hon." Andrew opened the door. "I'll pick you up on Tuesday."

She didn't press him further. His aloofness required no explanation.

"Jessica." Doctor Andrew Harrison grasped her arm.

His grief no longer hidden, she drew a breath slowly. It would take little for Jessica to cry.

"Honey, your grandfather loved you more than life itself. You were his whole world. Don't ever forget that." Andrew withdrew his hand and placed it in his pants pocket.

Jessica kissed his cheek. The old character would find it too much to handle, but she did it anyway. Closing the door, Jessica descended the stairs to the car.

"Where to now, M'lady? Your chariot awaits."

"Home." Delaying the inevitable was doing little to reduce her anxiety. "But first, stop by the funeral home so I can pick up my Jeep."

Putting the car in gear, Steven drove around the circular lane to the street.

"Andrew seemed...I don't know...strange?"

"He just lost his best friend, Jess." Steven paused. "Which brings up the question...why wasn't he at the funeral?"

"Jonas and Andrew swore to each other they would not attend the other's funeral. It was the last memory they held of their wives, a pain they never overcame and one they preferred not to experience again." An all but audible laughter escaped.

"Why is that funny?" Steven's creased brow confirmed his confusion with the amused reaction.

"Well, Jonas always said 'Andrew was too ornery to die.'" Jessica pushed at the lump rising in her throat. "And Andrew..." She bit her lip. "Andrew said 'Jonas was too stubborn.'" She felt the trembling, the hollow void. "I'm really going to miss those two..." The extent of loss reached beyond her control.

Steven, pulling up beside Jessica's Jeep, let the stillness serve its purpose.

"Follow me home?" Jessica hopped in the Wrangler, revved the engine and headed towards the farm.

***

The fire had dwindled. Wood sat stacked neatly to the right of the hearth. He placed a piece of hickory then oak onto the glowing embers. The fire danced to life.

"Oh child." Andrew's voice fell into the hush of the room. *Thank God for Steven.*

Since childhood, wherever there had been Jessica, Steven wasn't too far behind. *That boy had better stick around for a while. She would need him now more than ever.*

He'd been prepared for her to question him more. It was not Jessica's nature to accept things so willingly.

She hadn't picked up on the oddity of two executors on such a limited estate. One heir did not usually require so much assistance. She was obviously too worn down from the events of the last few days to notice.

He had to make it to the reading of the will. There he prayed he would find a better idea of what to tell her.

The years had not lessened the agony or dimmed the vivid images of that night.

How Jonas kept it so well hidden testified to the devotion he had for his grandchild. That deep abiding love had been the source of his strength. And his obsession to protect Jessica finally took Jonas McCabe's life.

Andrew looked deep into the red and orange flames.

She was going to demand answers. His mission, keep the promise, no matter how close she got. He would not let it destroy another life.

Up until the night Jonas died, Andrew had remained steadfast in his commitment to keep the secret safe. The final conversation between them now had Andrew second-guessing the long ago decision.

He ran his wrinkled hand across his brow, following his unshaven jaw line to his rough whiskered chin. "Lord, Jonas, what did you need to tell me?"

CHAPTER 4

The red sports car followed Jessica's well-traveled Jeep into the lane. The descending afternoon sun gleamed in the west windows of the house. The desire to run away was strong, but the place to run to was here.

Her eyes traveled to the barn and machine shed that bordered the farm on the north and east. The barn housed her grandfather's veterinarian practice and office. The machine shed stored the lawn tractor, tools and the equipment used in his work.

Straight ahead was the cattle lot and hog barn, which Jonas had used to board patients.

South of the hog barn was the chicken coop. He'd kept chickens as a hobby, sharing the extra eggs with neighbors.

In the southeast corner, the farm's original corncrib.

Her grandfather had been a stickler about keeping the acreage maintained, evidenced by the well-kept buildings and neatly trimmed lawn.

The garage anchored the south edge of the acreage. It

had a new electric overhead door installed this past spring. Jessica demanded it after the original heavy wooden one had come off its tracks and nearly killed Jonas.

On the west edge of the acreage sat the farmhouse, painted a crisp white with forest green shutters accenting each window. A wide porch wrapped around three sides. It had served as her castle, playhouse, a ship sailing the seas. Jessica held dear the many childhood adventures experienced on the huge expanse that hugged the white house.

A large, two-story home with a walk up attic, it afforded more than enough space for two people. Yet, the house was never overwhelming, but instead cozy and inviting. It was home.

A furry mug smeared the window of the office with its wet nose. Harvey. *Poor fella.* He'd been in there the entire day.

Jessica wondered how he would adjust to the loss of his companion.

When Andrew discovered her grandfather that morning, Harvey sat with his head on Jonas' lap. Andrew had told Jessica on the phone he was certain the dog hadn't moved a muscle since it happened.

Harvey, at the end of the lane when Jessica had gotten home on Wednesday afternoon, wagged his tail and ran to the driver's side first. Then, expecting Jonas, he dashed to the passenger side of the Jeep. But no one got out.

Jessica watched, helpless, as the dog returned to the top step of the porch, half in half out of the sun.

She had sat by Harvey, rubbing his coat of brown and

white fur until the sun had set. The sky and its limitless expanse tried to lift their spirits with a colorful display of pinks, oranges, purples, reds and blues. But, the sun in all its grandeur could do little for such heavy hearts.

That evening as the moon had come out to light the way for its nightly visitors, Jessica had gotten up and Harvey followed. Ending up in the living room both in front of the T.V., Jessica stared at the screen, seeing nothing, as movies played throughout the night.

This morning as she dressed to leave, Harvey lay at the foot of the bed, forlorn. She had buried her nose in his dense coat, whispering an assurance. She then put Harvey in the clinic office, easing the fear she had that he would follow her.

Jessica unlocked the office, and the big dog bounded out toppling her to the ground. A mutt in the truest sense, the dog verged on equestrian in size.

Harvey washed away any trace of makeup and covered her skirt with muddy paw prints. There was no anger.

Steven climbed out of his car and walked to the two sitting on the ground, mud and all. "What about me, Harv fella?" Steven kneeled and received his own personal greeting.

Jessica peered briefly into the office. Harvey hadn't disturbed anything.

She came into the sunlight, locking the door again. Jessica had not been able to bring herself to go into the office, he'd suffered his stroke here, but that was not the reason.

Some of Jessica's most treasured memories were Jonas working in his office. Whether caring for an animal, or poring over the latest developments in veterinarian medicine, he was most at home here.

This place was the hardest to deal with.

His love for his chosen profession had inspired Jessica to become a vet. It had thrilled Jonas, who never missed a chance to brag about his granddaughter the veterinarian.

Sharing the practice before he retired had been Jessica and Jonas' dream.

But she needed to be on her own for a while. And Jonas had understood, as it served also as an escape from what she had not been ready to confront.

Even now, the uncertainty was there. Could she deal with it, overcome it?

Fortunately, the University had a research position at the time of her graduation. Located 75 miles east of Gracier, it was close enough to come home for a weekend yet far enough away for the young vet to maintain her own identity.

They had talked that maybe by next spring. She had struggled. Longing to come home battled the anxiety of living up to Jonas' reputation. Now it had come without choice, sooner than expected.

She turned away from her inherited legacy.

"Hey, you," Steven, kneeling next to Harvey, rose. "Any libations in there?"

Harvey bounded up the steps.

The back entry served as both mudroom and laundry room. To the right, the door to the basement, to the left was the washer and dryer. A sink for washing stood left of the doorway into the kitchen.

Jonas and Jessica had always done the housekeeping themselves until she had landed the position at the University. After a little coaxing, he had hired Carlotta to come out one day a week. It had eased Jessica's mind.

The home's welcoming atmosphere was purely Jonas, doing everything in his power to insure Jessica had a normal home life despite the absence of the typical nuclear family. She couldn't think of a time when the kitchen air didn't dance with the aroma of home cooked meals, oatmeal raisin cookies, his specialty, or dark, rich rye bread.

She entered the kitchen's great expanse and inhaled, hoping to experience the smell of one last, fresh baked memory.

Steven at the refrigerator surveyed for promising contents.

"Not positive what's all in there?" Jessica laid her keys and purse on the counter. "It's well stocked though." Jonas was ready for whomever and whatever arrived.

Jessica, on tiptoes, glanced over Steven's shoulder. "Why don't you grab one for me, and I'll meet you in the front room."

She headed up the backstairs and down the hall to her bedroom. The west window let in the last remnants of the day.

Tugging off her dress and pantyhose, she sighed. *Finally.* She could usually come up with an excuse for not wearing dress clothes, but today had warranted no exceptions.

Crossing the cool wood floor to the chest of drawers, Jessica found a t-shirt and a pair of Levi's. The attire triggered an immediate release of tension.

Picking the brush up from the top of the dresser, she sat on the four-poster bed and brushed the tangles. Grabbing a hair clasp, Jessica pulled her mane into a controllable tail. Her gaze went out the west windows as the darkness chased away the daylight cloaking the distant horizon. This day was done.

"Jessica?" Steven interrupted her wandering thoughts. "Hey Jess, are you all right up there?"

"I'm coming." Jessica slid from the bed's high perch to the floor. Leaning against the oak dresser, she put on a pair of oversized socks for warmth against the night air. The final layer a sweatshirt, its plush interior against her skin, soothing. A true simple pleasure.

Jessica descended the front stairs leading to the entry foyer.

To the right, the living room and in his usual perch on the overstuffed couch, Steven.

"Now this girl seems familiar?" Steven folded his arms assessing her appearance. "Why it's Jessica McCabe!"

Jessica bowed at the introduction then crossed the room to her favorite chair and ottoman, dropping into its worn welcoming leather with a sigh.

"Cinderella has returned." The first hint of melancholy. A phrase Jonas had said to her as she raced up the stairs to remove her "Sunday finery" and don dungarees, now sounded hollow.

"Collapse is more like it," Steven commented. "After this one, you and I outta hit the road. Mom will be holding dinner for us."

"I'm not really up for any socializing, thanks anyway." Jessica eased slightly at the steady comfort of Steven, wanting to take care of his little sister. "Harvey and I are hanging here tonight."

"You okay out here?" Steven's legs dangled at one end of the sofa. His head propped on the other. "Why, we could have a slumber party. My car parked here all night." He raised his eyebrows, daring her. "The grapevine would be smokin'."

"We'll be fine." Jessica shook her finger at him scolding the attempted antics.

Steven's head and shoulders sank, mimicking disappointment.

"Where were you on assignment?"

"You'll get a real kick out of this one..." Steven cleared his throat, a signal to the gravity of his latest venture. "D.C., covering 'Pets of the Washington Elite'."

Jessica couldn't hide her amusement. "What in the world were you doing there? I thought you were covering the elections."

"Well I...I got myself into a little hot water and as a reprimand my editor sent me to do the Washington Elite's Annual Pet Show for Charity." Toasting with his beer bottle, he saluted. "If only those critters could talk."

Jessica's side ached at his knack for getting into trouble.

Steven had been interested in photography ever since his parents bought him his first 35mm in junior high. From then on, no matter the event, Steven would be there, camera in tow.

Neatly arranged in albums, she couldn't begin to imagine how many pictures he had taken.

In college, he'd gone into photojournalism and soon became known on campus for always getting "the shot" for the school newspaper. From the winning touchdown, showing the player's toes just inside the line, to campus police breaking up an out of control frat party, Steven got his shot. Jessica was amazed at his ability to be in the right place at the right and sometimes wrong, time.

After graduation, portfolio in hand, he called on all the major publications, landing a job at *Viewpoint*, an up and coming magazine, quickly earning a reputation for its coverage of controversial issues.

Government coup, civil rights marches, presidential election. They were recognized as "cutting edge" in the periodical industry.

She recalled his excitement when he landed the job. Steven found what he was looking for, and *Viewpoint* had a photojournalist who wasn't afraid to get what they wanted.

"What in the world did you do to deserve such an assignment?" Jessica had finally contained her laughter. "The magazine covers that stuff?"

"No they don't, but my editor decided I could help out one of our *sister* publications. Old news. How's the veterinarian research business doing, Doc?"

He knew what it meant to Jessica to be called Doc. The look of appreciation confirmed it.

"It's been good. In fact, I'd been thinking about finishing my research, taking the plunge and moving back in the spring." Jessica measured Steven's response.

"Well, this kind of speeds that decision up a little bit." Steven finishing a drink of his beer, kicked his shoes off and plopped his feet on the end table. He wasn't too worked up about his mother or dinner.

Jessica's thoughts shifted to the wall filled with pictures of her, infancy to young adulthood.

Jonas had captured the special moments on film and displayed his favorites throughout the house.

Her eyes went to the one showing college graduation, holding her degree. She wished Jonas had stood beside her in the picture instead of taking it.

That day they had discussed Jessica joining the practice after completing her work at the University research clinic in Harden.

Jonas had patiently waited, ready for her take over. Now he would not be there to pass the reins. Instead, he had left them lying there for Jessica to pick up, alone.

"Jessica...earth to Jessica," Steven cajoled her into the present. "Woman, you haven't heard a brilliant word I've said."

"I'm sorry. It's just, to run the practice... his practice. I wonder..." Jessica couldn't finish the thought.

"Wonder, nothing!" Steven was upright. "Who is the woman who has always known exactly what she wanted to do, when she wanted to do it, and never doubted for a second if it could be done?"

Picking up his nearly empty beer bottle, he pointed the long neck in his own direction. "And who in this relationship has been the one confused by the bigger picture, the 'where is life taking me' issue?" He looked at her in mock bewilderment. "Don't change course on me now, sister. This dog is too old to be learnin' new tricks."

She failed in her attempt to remain unamused with his self-deprecation. But Steven wasn't finished.

"Jess, your dream was to practice here. You've talked about it ever since I can remember." He made a wide arc with his hand. "It's where you're meant to be." He halted, thrown by the unprecedented role as counselor in the longtime relationship.

She was so lucky to have him.

"What are you afraid of?" He hesitated.

She recognized he was careful not to push.

"Jess...you can do this. You know it, I know it and Jonas knew it. It was his dream as much as it--"

"I used to have a lot of dreams, Steven. But they aren't always meant to come true are they?" She let the pause confirm that he understood the reference.

"Besides, who's to say people are willing to accept a woman as their vet. I'm not Jonas. Those are shoes I wouldn't pretend to be able to fill."

"Give me a break." Steven thudded his beer bottle on the table. "Jessica, you've been Jonas' shadow since the day you could walk! His extra set of hands! Or better yet, can you even count the number of people at your graduation reception who asked how long before the sign would read 'Dr. Jessica McCabe?'" Steven smirked triumphantly. "Need I say more?"

"No, you need not say more," Jessica rebuked, irritated her insecurities deemed trivial. "It was supposed to be him and me--" her voice caught, the weight of sadness undeniable, "at least for awhile."

The hidden apprehension crept in, "Besides, there are people around here who would be quite content if I never returned and this land went up for sale."

The muscles in his tanned jaw tightened. He spoke slowly and deliberately, "The Cassidys have *nothing* to do with this."

It simmered just below the boiling point, the sometimes dormant, but never extinct volcano regarding the Cassidy family, the eruption from Mt. Steven inevitable.

"I don't care if they want the land. It wouldn't be up for sale whether you stayed and practiced or not, it is a 'non-issue'." Steven took a drag of beer, the last in the bottle, working hard to regain his control.

She noted her appreciation without speaking.

The Cassidys, buying up land for years, had succeeded in acquiring almost every available acre adjacent to the McCabe farm.

And Joseph Cassidy unyielding, had boasted he would someday own the farm as well. His arrogance on the subject had served to fuel many heated exchanges between Jonas and the self-serving lawyer. Jessica had experienced it firsthand.

At home though, it was a family joke. *"How much Cassidy Cash are we worth today?"* Jonas had quipped when land prices went up or down or the crops were exceptionally good.

Steven noticed the happiness as it lit up Jessica's face. Something, for a moment was okay.

He had etched this vision, the curve of her mouth, the arch of her beautiful brow into his mind's eye. He held it there, ready, whenever faraway, to ease the emptiness that only she could fill. *Reel it in, brother!*

His beer gone, Steven stood up and stretched, his fingers just short of touching the ceiling.

His height had served him well in school athletics, but had gotten him in some tight situations in his overseas shoots. When avoiding sniper fire or hostile crowds, being a six foot five inch brown haired, blue-eyed American was not a good thing.

"Another one?" Jessica grabbed the empty.

"I better go." Steven bent to put his shoes on. "She'll have the 'Art patrol' out on me shortly."

The deployment of Steven's father to round up the troops was a leftover from childhood. From backyards to the Gracier swimming pool, a honk from the family station wagon had put the fear of God in the Conrad kids on more than one occasion. Steven wasn't sure if his father's irritation at the duty was authentic or if it actually served as an escape, putting distance between himself and his wife's ruffled feathers.

"The folks would *love* to see you?"

"And I bet you would *love* your old buddy Jessica to play defense when it comes to Mother Conrad's famous mealtime inquisition of her number one son."

Steven pretended to be taken aback. She'd hit the nail on the head. His mother was relentless in her pursuit of information.

Jessica winked, amused at what he had yet to endure. "Really Steven, I'm tired. Tell your mom 'Hi' for me though. I saw her at church helping the ladies serve, but we never got a chance to talk."

Reaching the porch, Steven pushed the screen door then stepped back against the doorframe. "Call if you need anything. I don't care what it is or--"

She wrapped her arms around him. "My anchor in a storm."

Delivering his best captain's salute Steven took the steps two at a time and crossed the farmyard to his car. *Please Art have something strong in the liquor cabinet and keep Mother Conrad preoccupied while I find it.*

***

The little red sports car drove down the lane and into town. She walked into the kitchen to find Harvey by the cupboard where they kept his dog food.

She pulled a pot pie from the freezer and popped it in the oven. Then ran a can of dog food under the electric can opener and spooned the contents into Harvey's dog dish. Bit by bit, he devoured his supper.

In the living room, switching on the set, she began to

click aimlessly. She didn't remember dosing off.

CHAPTER 5

"BEEP! BEEP! BEEP!"

Jessica sprang from the chair, trying to focus, the T.V. her only light. Her foggy mind tried to grasp where she was, which way the ear shattering noise originated from and the source of the burnt crust smell...*the pot pie*!

She ran into the smoke-filled kitchen. Throwing the oven open, Jessica grabbed the dishtowel hanging on the kitchen chair. The smoke billowed, stinging her eyes. The round, black, smoking lump held little resemblance to a pot pie. Racing out the door, she tossed the smoldering supper onto the gravel lane.

Back in the kitchen, Jessica went first to the south window, then to the west windows, opening them wide to let the smoke out. Finally, she switched on the ceiling fan, appeasing the alarm.

Flopping on the floor beside Harvey, who had also been startled out of a deep sleep, she began to rub the dog's belly.

"Well, I wasn't hungry anyway."

The grandfather clock in the foyer chimed eight o'clock. She panned the room. Truth be told she was not in the mood to spend another night sitting in the house.

"Harv, let's go."

The dog's ears perked up as he danced around, anxiously awaiting Jessica.

Jessica retrieved a pullover jacket then slipped on her shoes. "Now listen bud, you're right by me, no running off okay?"

Harvey cocked an ear in acknowledgment. They headed out into the night.

The McCabe acreage was about one and a half miles out on the east edge of town, the road into town gravel, until the last half mile where it met the city limits and became black top.

Jessica and Harvey jogged for a while. Formerly an early morning ritual, the hectic schedule of the last few years had not permitted much jogging.

Few in number, the lights of downtown Gracier cast a halo into the fall sky. The stars overhead sparkled. The full moon, a night watchman, lit the dim corners of the crisp autumn evening.

Except for a half a dozen layers of black top and some patched potholes, the road had stayed the same. Still, Harvey sniffed out every dirt clump that had fallen from a car's wheel well. Once in awhile his curiosity would stir up a bird and normally he would take chase until it flew over a fence line. Tonight, the old farm dog tended to be at her heel.

Jessica kicked some pebbles, scattering the gravel. A cat

slinked across the road ahead, avoiding Harvey's observant eye.

On this bright October evening, the outlines of trees and buildings were visible for miles. Serene silhouettes as day melted to night.

They entered the city limits. *Man, there were a lot of cars?* Then it registered...*Saturday night.*

She looked at her faithful companion. "Well Harvey, I guess it's you and me. Ready for a wild night on the town?"

Harvey barked his approval.

There would be a lot of people out tonight enjoying the beautiful fall weather. Walking was a favorite pastime for many in this small community.

As they came to Main Street, Jessica caught sight of Gracier's town square. She was not particularly interested in all the hubbub. But, she was interested in a Diet Pepsi and the nearest source happened to be a pop machine outside the front of Cooper's Grocery.

Harvey seemed thrilled at the choice of direction.

Gracier's main street consisted of large homes on both the north and south ends. The business district, surrounding the town square, sat right in the middle of this main thoroughfare. The four blocks of store fronts facing it were neat and tidy, a sign of proud Midwest heritage. Jessica took solace in her hometown's familiarity.

The pop machine outside Cooper's Grocery glowed, calling to those craving some refreshment. A group of moths hovered around its illuminated letters.

Jessica dug into her pocket. "Damn." Nothing there, she

checked her two back pockets. "I swear I put fifty cents in here..." Reaching into her front left pocket, she found a dollar bill. "Well fella, you're going to have to wait outside the bar while I go in for change, okay?"

They walked the street to Mickey's Bar and Grill, one of three local bars, and a popular hangout for young and old alike on Saturday night.

"You stay, boy." She yanked the heavy wood door and stepped inside to a world of music and laughter.

The booming voice cut the din, "Angel!"

Jessica walked the length of the oak and brass railed bar to where Mickey stood by the register ringing out a customer.

He finished his tally, wiped his hands, and came out from behind. A huge man with a barrel chest, Mickey's arms testified to his years of lifting kegs and drunks as owner of this fine establishment.

Mickey, or Michael Hansen, as the local sheriff knew him, had always taken a special interest in Jessica. One of her mother's best friends growing up, he had always been there for "Maggie's Little Angel".

Oddly enough, he rarely spoke of her.

"Two fingers of whiskey and a beer chaser, barkeep." She held up two fingers mischievously sizing up the order. But there would be no liquor served to Jessica by this barkeep, no matter what the age. Overprotective was an understatement.

Mickey's massive arms went around her. "You are a sight for sore eyes. All I ever get to see are these old boys." He tipped his head to the nightly cast of hometown characters lining the bar stools.

They responded with a few whoops and smart-ass remarks before returning to their own conversations.

Mickey set Jessica on the floor again. The gentle giant's width magnified his six foot three inch stance. "Are you doing okay?" His bearded face had drawn into a troubled frown.

Jessica accepted the concern and the comfort it gave her tired soul. It had been too long. "I saw you today, but I didn't really get a chance... it meant a lot, Mick." She gave her favorite ruddy, red whiskered Irishman a kiss.

Hoots of delight and fun loving harassment filled the small bar.

Mickey blushed and then hoisted his immense paw at the crowd. All present knew better than to go any further.

"Have you been eating? Sleeping?" He motioned to a stool at the bar inviting Jessica to sit.

"I can't, Mickey." Jessica pulled the dollar from her pocket. "Harvey's outside."

"Bring him in." Mickey jutted a thick thumb indicating an area under the counter behind the bar.

"Isn't that illegal?" She smirked. His personal concern for the law was not a priority. Never had been, never would be.

"That dog has sat in here while Jonas played cards with Chester Caughlin for umpteen years. If the former Sheriff doesn't mind then I would say we're safe. Now go get him."

Jessica went to the front and signaled for Harvey to come.

Tail wagging, he trotted to his customary location behind the bar, spun around twice and laid down curled in a circle.

"Now, sit and tell me how you're doing."

Jessica slid up onto the dark brown leather barstool with its four steel legs. Worn to a soft luster they were still steady and solid.

"Well, if I can't have a whiskey, a Diet Pepsi will do." Jessica laid the crumpled dollar on the bar.

Mickey pushed it away. "First, a burger with the works and fries, then you can have your pop." Mickey marched into the kitchen.

Jessica tucked the dollar into her jeans.

In the mirror behind the bar, she assessed the occupants of the usual assigned seats.

Mickey's was filled, typical for a Saturday night. A good portion of Hannah's congregation spent their evening hours here on the weekends.

And when someone, not a regular, came in, they stuck out like a sore thumb. Jessica held the distinction of tonight's sore thumb.

Mickey came out from the kitchen. "Your supper is cooking. Now I'll set you up." Taking a glass, he filled it with ice-cold pop. "This is better for you than 13 year old whiskey."

"Thank you sir." Picking up the glass, Jessica gulped its contents, thirsty from the jaunt.

"Good Lord Child," Mickey turned around from pouring an order. "Haven't you been drinking either?" He topped off her drink.

"Mick, I have a kitchen at home." She paused, not sure if the big man behind the bar was listening as he strode, one end to the other, filling up and dumping out.

"Yep, and I'd lay money on the fact you haven't cooked a meal yet, let alone been eating right." Mickey scolded gently.

This was an argument she had no chance of winning, so wisely she switched subjects. "Looks like all the regulars are here. Except for a few here and there, I recognize everybody."

Grabbing a group of used glasses with his large burly hands, he plunged them into the sink. Wisps of steam slipped between the mass of white suds into the air. "Well, a couple are missing, but most of the gang's here." The tumbler Mickey scrubbed was getting quite a once over, the usually outspoken bartender uncomfortable with his unintentional reference to Jonas.

She needed him to know it was okay. "Nobody playing cards tonight?" Jessica had noted Chester and Jonas' absence long before Mickey referred to it. "I'm going give that table some company."

Mickey lifted his head and smiled. "I'll bring out your food as soon as it's up and join you." The Irishman gestured towards the young man waiting on customers at the other end of the bar. "Pete can manage this for awhile."

Jessica carried her drink to the empty table under the bar light. Four chairs, worn to a mellow, honey color surrounded it. The table's smooth Formica top made it easy to slide cards dealt in the weekly Saturday night games.

Sitting down Jessica began to observe the bar's activities, having unconsciously perched in the exact manner Jonas used to.

People waved. She returned the welcome.

Harvey's sad expression begged for permission.

She patted her leg, the signal clear.

Crossing the room, he crawled beneath the table, this time next to Jessica's feet.

"Here you go. Burger, all the trimmings, fries and coleslaw. Now eat. Give me a minute and I'll keep you company." Mickey's giant stride had him half way across the bar before she could utter a thanks.

Jessica had to admit the mound of food smelled pretty good. She tipped the ketchup bottle Mickey had set on the table until a satisfactory amount of her favorite condiment filled the plate. Wading a couple of fries through the pool of ketchup, she savored a healthy bite.

"Overcome our ketchup addiction, I see."

Jessica wiped the self-induglence from her mouth with a napkin. His tall frame towered.

"Mind if I keep you company while you eat?"

She nodded.

Matthew pulled the chair out. "Quite a meal you've got there."

"Well, Mickey's idea of healthy portions is different than most." Jessica worked to keep the conversation light and distant.

Matthew's deep, emerald eyes shone in spite of the dimly lit room.

Her heart beat faster. *Why was it still so hard?*

Wavy, raven black hair trimmed up over his ears, above his collar, framed chiseled features tanned from a season working the land.

"Mind if I have a fry?"

"There's plenty here."

He retrieved the golden deep fat fried side dish. Toned from farming his hand, despite the work, appeared gentle.

Jessica glanced up. He did not yield, focused in an all too familiar way.

Unsettled, Jessica reached down to check on Harvey sitting under the table, willing herself to look away. "Want some, boy?" The hungry mutt devoured the fry in one bite.

"Hey, boy." Matthew patted his knee.

Tail wagging furiously, Harvey stuck his head up and laid it in Matthew's lap.

"You've gained a new friend."

An awkward silence, Jessica preferred to avoid, filled the air.

"Well, I can pretty much guess what you're going to say to my offer." He traced the random patterns of the glossy Formica tabletop. "But I'll take the risk."

There it was, in her gut, a red flag. Her intuition never failed. She had regretfully chosen to ignore it on several occasions. Not tonight.

"If you need a couple of hands around the farm I'll be more than happy to help." He took another fry. "So don't be afraid to ask."

He was fishing. She knew his bait and switch better than

anyone. No doubt, it served Gracier's hotshot young lawyer well in the courtroom.

"I appreciate the offer," Jessica salted the layer of fries, "but I can handle it okay."

"You're keeping the farm aren't you?"

Ah yes, there it was, his true motive. Like his father, he was in it for himself.

"Well, you have company, Jess. Hungry, Mr. Cassidy? Can I getcha' a burger?"

Matthew raised a hand to Mickey's hospitality. "No Sir, I'm just fine."

"He can have what's left of mine." Jessica shoved her chair back. "Mick, you're a peach, but it's late and I'm tired." She squeezed one of his calloused hands. "Come on, Harv."

Matthew stood up, the look of bewilderment, Oscar worthy. "Jess, what did I--"

"Let me by, Matthew." Jessica couldn't stand the proximity and the unmistakable betrayal.

"Jessica!"

Half way up the street, with Harvey at her side, Jessica's pace quickened at the sound of her name.

***

His truck drove up beside them, windows rolled down.

"So this is how it's going to be!" his deep voice outdid the rumbling engine.

"Go home Matthew." Anger fueled Jessica's determined gait. "Go home to your family. Tell your father I'm not selling, so the vultures can stop swarming."

The pickup stopped. He was directly in Jessica's path. She stepped off the sidewalk to go around him, but Matthew had her shoulders, his grip firm.

She didn't know whether to be more upset by the way he was forcing her to stand there or his presence still shaking her to the core.

His hands relaxed, but rested on Jessica's shoulders. He was not letting go until she heard what he had to say.

Jessica's eyes burned, her throat thickened. *Damn it!* She bit her lip to contain the hurt and anger searching for a way to escape.

"Matthew, get back in your truck. There is nothing you can say--"

"Jessica, I'm *not* my father."

He was measuring what he should say. *On your toes, McCabe.*

"I asked about the farm because I'm worried about you."

His eyes registered with...pain? Hurt? The intensity could be mesmerizing. Jessica focused on the mantra that had kept her steady. *He made his choice, and it wasn't you.* "You mean you're worried about the land."

A brief shadow of anger crossed Matthew's face.

She had hit the mark.

"I was never involved in his business dealings, land or otherwise. Why do you let others--?"

"It has nothing to do with others, Matthew. It has to do with me. Even after all that happened, I still believed you weren't him. Wrong again, wasn't I?"

He removed his hands and walked to the pickup.

She should be thrilled, vindicated. She'd gotten the last word. Instead, affirmation of his guilt settled like a weight in the pit of Jessica's stomach.

He stopped, his hand on the hood, "I mean it Jess, I'm here day or night." He climbed in and drove away.

"Come on boy." Harvey was at her heel. She was not sure how her arms or legs were working. "Damn it!" Jessica's profanity cut the night air and disappeared into the darkness.

***

Matthew gasped for air, the anguish overtaking him. Bile rose in his throat. Pulling off the road, he jumped out, his body retching uncontrollably.

The hatred, the loathing, she despised him. For her to believe he had followed in his father, Joseph Cassidy's, arrogant self-serving footsteps was too much. But Matthew had done an amazing job convincing her.

And now he had all but defied Jessica to stay, challenged her to prove herself. It had not been his intention, though to hold her...to touch her. He knew better. The promise, keeping her beyond, racked his body once again.

Matthew's thoughts went to Jonas McCabe. *How did he bear it?* The resolve, unshaken, evident whenever he spoke Jessica's name, a granddaughter he would protect at all costs. Now the love Matthew held within would have to be his strength, as it had been for Jonas. The young lawyer's consolation, Jonas' tired soul was now free.

The burden was his alone.

***

Jessica lay in bed exhausted, begging her mind to shut off and let long awaited sleep bring comfort. She searched for a reason to trust him. Her heart joined in the battle, telling Jessica again to believe.

CHAPTER 6

Sunday morning came with sunshine and not a cloud in the sky, a "postcard day" as Jonas would say.

Father O'Malley offered Mass for Jonas. It was the reason she had come.

Many family friends greeted Jessica upon entering the dark brick church. The week's tension eased as she observed the antics of the latest generation of Cooper children seated in the front pew.

Mass concluded, Jessica headed to the farm, got both her and Harvey a little lunch and decided to tackle the office.

She started across the lane to the barn. The sign over the door read:

JONAS MCCABE, VETERINARIAN.

If she decided to continue the practice, she would add her name below.

The office occupied one corner of the red barn where he boarded animals for specialized treatment. At the time of his death, there were no patients in his care.

Jessica inserted the key in the lock. Fresh hay, antiseptic, her grandfather's aftershave...to this farm girl the scent of home, of everything right.

She opened the window allowing the fall breeze in to push away the mustiness that had settled in the room.

The worn, wooden planked floor traced the pattern of his days. She followed it to the chair. His chair, brown leather worn to a supple bronze, its rich smell reminding Jessica of the owner.

Sitting there, Jessica's mind raced back to a child running in and out of the barn, bringing injured kittens, mice and even crickets for Jonas to fix.

In his gentle hands, he would tend to the wounded critters and Jessica would be out the door on the hunt for another patient.

Jessica relished the memory. The office now brought more comfort than anywhere else she could imagine.

The unkept desk she had not anticipated.

Papers and bills were stacked to one side, descending in an avalanche to the middle of the honey hued oak desk. Jonas' chipped coffee cup sat on the edge, stained from years of use and all too little washing.

Jessica thumbed through the bills and invoices. Some were paid, some were not, and some were barely legible.

The hours ticked by as she sorted the stacks of paperwork and gradually, the harsh reality sank in, something had been wrong for much longer than she suspected.

The thought of him suffering, hiding it from everyone, except for perhaps, one person. If anyone, he could shed light on what Jonas' office had revealed.

***

The call had come sooner than expected.

Doctor Andrew Harrison removed the reading glasses perched upon his nose and placed them on the desk. He folded the Sunday paper he'd been struggling to read, his mind somewhere else.

He had promised him, if, and when she started to ask, he would hold fast to what they had agreed. The only thing worse than the secret was the truth.

The weight Jonas had carried somewhat lifted with the formation of the Land Corporation. Unfortunately, the consolation it brought was short-lived.

Finding him that morning, Andrew had little doubt the years of secrecy had finally taken their toll.

"I've made a terrible mistake, Andrew."

Jonas' statement from that night on the phone had weighed heavy on his mind. He should have gone out to the farm then instead of waiting until the morning. But Jonas, adamant, said he had things to take care of, alone.

Dr. Andrew Harrison knew his friend had struggled with not telling Jessica more about the partners and the land deal. Nevertheless, it was too late.

The knock brought him to the promise to keep.

The two walked to the front room, each taking a seat in the overstuffed chairs that anchored either side of the fireplace.

Andrew had started a fire, hoping to get the fall chill out of his old bones.

Leaning forward, elbows on her knees, Jessica stared into the flames.

Andrew waited to begin the conversation he would never be quite ready for.

"Why didn't he tell me?" She paused. "Why didn't you tell me?" Her voice was not accusing, but instead one of sadness and regret.

"You knew your grandfather better than anyone, Jessica. Admit something was wrong? Hell, he wouldn't even come in for an exam." Andrew stopped.

She blamed herself, but no one besides his few close friends had detected any significant change. The stubborn old man hid it well. He had hidden it all quite well.

Now it was up to Andrew.

"Why didn't I move home sooner?" Jessica's eyes welled. "Selfish...Andrew, to not see...?" Silent drops fell.

Andrew came forward. "Look at me."

Jessica's gaze met Andrew's.

"He didn't die because you weren't here." He held his composure, wanting to be the strength she could depend on in the days to come. "Jessica, he more than anyone, understood you needed some space."

The heartbreak, usually well hidden, swept Jessica. Space and time had done little to heal the young woman.

"He saved me Andrew...and I..." Jessica's speech tore with agony, "where was I when he needed me?"

"Jessica McCabe. I will not sit and watch you do this. He died a happy, ornery, stubborn cuss. And if he were here right now he would chew you up one side and down the other." His skin prickled, signaling the growing redness. It served in his purpose to convince her.

"Well I guess you and I are taking up where you and Jonas left off."

The smirk turning up the corners of Jessica's mouth eased the tension. "But remember Doctor, I've learned from the best."

They sat quietly.

"He asked if I needed help with anything."

Andrew didn't respond at first. Chester told him, Matthew's presence at the funeral had been hard on her.

"He's sincere, Jess." Andrew was treading on thin ice. "You can't blame him for his father's--"

"His father had nothing to do with his decision to walk away." Raw pain shone a hurt still fresh, not far below the surface.

The next few days were going to be harder than he'd imagined.

"You don't want to hear this, and I've got no room to talk, but there comes a time where you must forgive the past." Andrew reached over. "It will destroy you."

"The will is scheduled to be read at 10:00 Tuesday." Jessica's tone matter-of-fact, a not too subtle hint the topic was off-limits.

"Buried on a Saturday. Will read on a Tuesday. The two days Hannah serves rhubarb pie." Doctor Andrew Harrison chuckled. "Your grandfather promised the gang if he couldn't be there for pie, neither could they."

A smile tugged on the edges of her mouth.

"Ornery 'til the end and then some." For a moment, Andrew forgot the heartache he anticipated for Jess in the days to follow.

A hint of mischief flashed. "Can you put up with this McCabe?"

"I may be your elder, but those years provide me the much needed wisdom and true life lessons in how to handle a McCabe." He winked confidently.

Jessica stood up and kissed the top of his head. "Okay, Doc, you're on."

He felt the red travel up his neck. A tough old bird except when it came to her.

"Now, back to where I belong."

She was quiet until they got to the door.

"I'll see you in a couple days, if not before."

"Jessica, don't try to do it all at once." Andrew looked at her, so tired, so drained.

Jessica winked. "Who better to take care of the last surviving McCabe and that ever exasperating stubborn streak?"

The Jeep traveled out the drive. Beyond, the western horizon and the descending sun in all its brilliance introduced the night.

***

The black Iowa dirt turned as the plow cut releasing into the air a pungent smell causing nostrils to flare. Engulfing, it brought headiness to those who were lucky enough to experience it.

Matthew steered the tractor, leading the plow across the

end rows for another pass. The early morning sky had given way to a bright, intense fall sunshine and now the promise of a beautiful sunset as the dust and dirt hovering at the edge of the Iowa skyline mixed with its rays providing a glorious display.

He raised the plow. The tractor idled as he looked over his day's work. Matthew missed his grandfather the most on days like this.

Unlike his father Joseph, Matthew loved working the land alongside his grandfather. As a child, he would ride his bike out to the field, hop the fence and wave his arms as the John Deere chugged towards him.

People presumed he had chosen to follow in his father's footsteps. It couldn't be farther from the truth.

Matthew had originally gone to college seeking a degree in agriculture. Nevertheless, he soon found himself drawn to the course of study from which he had purposely stayed away.

Defying his father's wishes he returned home, determined to quit school, deny his true calling and join his grandfather in farming.

"Do you want to be an attorney, Matthew?" His *grandfather, sitting on an overturned feed bucket, pushed his green and gold hat back on his head.*

"If I do, he wins."

"If he keeps you from what you really want, doesn't he win anyway?"

The youngest Cassidy had his answer. Matthew

Cassidy's passion for farming was almost as great as his love for law.

The red barn broke the hill's crest. His father had inherited the acreage and the farm ground upon his grandfather's death.

Matthew's parents lived in town in a beautiful home they built. No one had lived out on the original homestead until Matthew moved back. He had convinced his father to rent the acreage to him, and he'd been there ever since.

One by one the farmhouse lights began to come on as dusk raced along the edge of the Iowa skyline. The McCabe farm sparkled, a small diamond of light to the south.

Last night did not go as planned. He kicked himself for pushing too far, too soon. It would take time to earn her trust, if he could regain it at all.

Heading into the house, he showered and dressed. Determined to undo the damage, Matthew drove down the gravel road leading him to the lights of the distant farmhouse.

sticking his wallet into his faded Levis.

"I got it." Matthew pointed to the checkbook in Jessica's hand. "But as long as you're writing checks, I could use a new--"

"Thanks, but you didn't need pay for my pizza," Jessica responded, irritated at his action. "I haven't had a chance to get any cash."

Pizza box in hand, Matthew walked to the kitchen with Harvey close behind, tail wagging furiously.

Jessica dropped the unused checkbook on the desk and followed them.

Entering the kitchen, she came upon Matthew laying a slab of pizza in Harvey's dog dish. "Well I'd say you've got a friend for life." Jessica reached into the cupboard for some plates. "Would you like to join me since you paid for it?" She knew the invitation was not expected. But she was taking Andrew's advice. She had to move on. She owned her future, no one else.

"Only if there's enough to spare." Matthew kept kneeling by the dog.

Jessica couldn't get over Harvey's friendly behavior. She set the plates on the counter behind Matthew.

"Nothing fancy tonight." Jessica opened the fridge. "Beer, pop, or milk...?"

"Beer would be fine." Matthew took the bottle. "Jess, I'm sorry for last night."

From the corner of her eye, she could see Matthew against the counter, head tipped, his thumb rubbing back and forth across the amber bottle.

"Are we okay with each other? Can we be?"

Jessica calmly taking the pizza box and a beer stepped out to the front porch.

He followed with the plates, obviously accepting her evasive response for now.

**

Producing deep hues of red and indigo, the sun departed into another world.

They both sat, seemingly involved in the pepperoni and mushrooms.

The moon began to take its audience in the sky, the glow of the evening lantern dancing among the folds of Jessica's dress.

It clung to her legs propped gracefully on the porch rail. Flowing to the porch floor, the warm night breeze briefly teased, drawing the dress up Jessica's tanned lean legs.

His eyes traveled to where the October moonlight illuminated the curve of her brow, the soft nape of her neck and he could not help but wish to take the woman into his arms.

Jessica suddenly faced him.

Matthew bit into his slice of pizza.

"So, you've become a scavenger."

"Let's just say the pizza delivery guy and I have an agreement."

Jessica was amused.

He hadn't been sure how she would react after last night, but he had to see her again before Tuesday.

"Another piece?" Jessica turned to offer a slice.

He looked first at the parted pink lips, then into her eyes. The intensity stopped just short of completely blinding him to the promise.

"Jess." He dug deep, his mind a fog. Desire rose, reason waned. Jonas' unflinching stare broke through the moment. *Damn it, this is not right.*

"Jess, I'm sorry, I..." He stopped. Taking a ragged breath, Matthew fought the urge to pull her close.

His heart broke as the flush of anticipation painted her cheeks. All she had refused to admit, now evident.

Jessica stood up.

Just a few more steps, let her go. "Jess." Matthew crossed the porch floor, taking her arm.

Her hand rested on door handle.

"I want--"

"You want what, Matthew?" Jessica's voice came out of their past shattering his resolve.

"You." He caressed her trembling lips with his for what he vowed would be the last time.

She stood rigid, refusing to reveal the turmoil inside.

Then the tear, its path a thin glistening trail, ended as it fell to the collar of his crisp blue shirt. The fabric gave at the rise and fall of his chest.

She battled the call, the hidden yearning that still believed in the man she loved...had loved.

His lights had faded into the night. She found the strength to move. The hollow victory was hers.

CHAPTER 8

Matthew didn't remember the drive to the bluff. As he slipped the pickup into park, his mind continued down the path, recalling the moment he'd seen Jessica for the beautiful young woman she had become and not the little girl he had teased relentlessly.

They had both grown up in this small Iowa town. Older than Jessica, she had been "the little McCabe girl" with a quick temper and equally quick wit. The combination had guaranteed a good laugh whenever the opportunity arose to play a prank. She in turn had the uncanny ability of repaying his efforts, when he least expected it.

It was during one of these classic confrontations that he became aware of the fact, the "little McCabe girl" she was no more.

It had been the summer he helped out in his father's law office on college break. The day was hot and humid, sending the heat index to a stifling 110 degrees, a typical July day in Iowa. He had decided to take the afternoon off and head out to the Lancaster County Fair.

Strolling the midway, he saw her smiling and waving at people as she darted in and out of the livestock buildings, helping her grandfather as usual, while also tending to her own animals.

4-H kids lived for this. Months of work waiting to be judged. And no one worked harder than Jess McCabe. Matthew suspected inborn tenacity with the extra incentive of being the granddaughter of the local vet.

Matthew had long ago heard the story of Jessi's grandfather, Jonas, and how he had raised the girl, as her mother, unwed, died shortly after giving birth to Jessica.

The young girl and her grandfather were a lot alike. And both had the respect of their peers. This said a lot about Jess, considering the decades of gossip.

Then there was Jonas McCabe, local veterinarian. A longstanding reputation in the community for giving selflessly both personally and professionally, Matthew knew of one person who didn't have the utmost respect for him.

The smell of cotton candy, the music piping from the merry-go-round and the screams from the Scrambler served to inspire even the most reserved midway observer to join in the fun. With this in mind, Matthew entered the livestock barn to see what he could do to make the little McCabe girl's 4-H experience a little more fun, at least from his perspective.

The opportunity presented itself too easily as he found Jessica in the barn rafters. An extension cord strung across the timbers, she was attempting to connect the cord to a small fan, which would help cool the cattle.

Waiting for Jessica to finish, to eliminate any risk, Matthew, with his hands on his hips, looked up at the precariously perched girl. "Always good to keep those cattle comfortable til you show'em."

Peeking cautiously over her shoulder, as not to lose balance and fall to the unforgiving cement below, Jessica smiled warily.

"Why if it isn't Judge Cassidy." She got a kick out of how the nickname galled him, evidenced by the smirk.

Matthew nodded acknowledging the sarcastic greeting. Jessica's triumph would be short lived.

As she crawled to where her cattle stood, tails swishing at the flies that droned above, Matthew crossed underneath, situating himself just right.

He raised his hand. "Here Miss McCabe, let me help you. That is no place for a young girl. If you fall you'll crack your skull."

Jessica eyed him suspiciously, undoubtedly questioning the trustworthiness of her adversary. "Thanks, but no thanks." She wiped a bead of sweat rolling to the end of her nose. "It may be hot, but it's not that hot." Jessica turned, backtracking to where she'd crawled up.

She stopped short as her grandfather's thundering bass resounded off the rafters, "Jessica Ann McCabe, what in the Sam Hill are you doing up there?"

Jonas McCabe then spotted Matthew standing below the rafters where his granddaughter teetered precariously. "Well, Matthew, lawyers have to be good for something in *this world."*

Matthew stood unfazed, despite the harsh comment. What he had in mind would be worth the verbal knock.

Jessica's hands in his, Matthew braced his feet helping her onto the fence between the stalls. Next to it, the water trough sat convenient for the livestock, as well as in this case, Matthew.

He held on until she had gained her balance on the fence. And as he suspected, she yanked away.

A grin broke across his face as her eyes filled with realization. She was falling backwards directly into the cattle trough full of lukewarm water, straw and assorted farm animal slobber.

Matthew stepped back anticipating the splash.

As he predicted, Jessica shot up from the trough as quickly as she had gone in. Eyes blazing, they would have stopped any man dead in his tracks.

That was not the reason for Matthew's stunned silence.

As if baptized in the water himself, Matthew Cassidy was rapt. Where moments before a girl, now stood a young woman.

Jessica's wet auburn hair clung to sun-kissed cheeks. Droplets of water ran down her shoulders, altering course ever so gently when meeting the rise in her chest, following the curve of a now wet and clinging 4-H t-shirt.

The water's descent continued to where the cropped shirt ended and the smooth, sunbathed torso, now exposed, glistened. Denim cut-offs clung to her wet hips, and the brown expanse of slender legs that followed disappeared into the water, leaving their soft slim beauty to his imagination. How long he stared, he did not know.

Luckily, Jessica's eyes saw nothing but red.

The anger they possessed served to return him to the project at hand.

Matthew reached for the fan mounted on the side of the stall and flipped the switch. "Fan works."

He walked out, leaving her standing in the trough, fists clenched, breathing fire.

As he broke into the light of early afternoon, he exhaled. The little McCabe girl she was not and what an incredible defiant beauty she had become. A lot had changed in four years.

The next day the sun shone just as brightly, shimmering off the silver top of Anderson's barber pole.

Striding down the street to the county courthouse, he carried under his arm papers to be delivered to the clerk's office.

Today was the end of the fair, and Main Street was host to as many pigs, sheep and cattle in livestock trailers as it was to farmers and trucks.

One particular trailer got his attention though, as he noticed Jessica McCabe and her high school friends sitting on the tailgate of her grandfather's Chevy.

An all too friendly wave triggered a trickle of apprehension. Oh, he was going to pay for yesterday.

He returned the greeting then continued, resolute, in the direction of the courthouse. His pace quickened, getting him away from the trouble he suspected would follow.

By the time he finished at the courthouse, it was afternoon. Descending the steps, Matthew, hungry, decided a J.J.'s Drive In burger and fries would do the trick.

Jumping in his pickup, he drove around the square and north on main. Two short blocks and the smell overcame him.

Pulling over he lifted the hood to find his prank repaid, sitting piled high and juicy on the manifold, a freshly baked cow pie.

The night air hinted of winter. He rolled up the window. It was late, but the memories she had unleashed kept him from firing the engine and driving home.

From the bluff, he could see the lights of the high-school football field twinkling a few miles away, an evening practice in session. East of the field were the county fairgrounds and livestock buildings. On the far side the fair barn.

It had been the last night of the fair when participants and fair goers attended the traditional 4-H dance. He had not admitted to himself why he had gone. The memory of Jessica dancing across the expanse of the fair barn would not let him forget.

Unlike most girls her age, Jess, more often than not, was in the company of older folks. Visiting with her grandfather's friends or coaxing one to dance to the latest hit was more her style.

She was mature beyond her age.

Distracted by the popping firecrackers outside the barn window, he didn't see Jessica until it was too late.

Hair, usually tied back, swirled loosely, tumbling across her shoulders. Her Levis fit perfectly. The white cotton blouse blew too easily in the breeze from the windows, exposing a beautiful, tanned neck and shoulders.

"Judge Cassidy." She was the epitome of the cat who swallowed the canary. "What may I ask allows us the honor of your presence?"

"Why Miss McCabe, I was fortunate enough to stumble upon someone's misplaced manure and thought perhaps the owner would be searching for it. What better place to look than a barn."

Her demeanor, innocent bystander, classic Jess.

"It's a shame when people can't keep track of their own bull shit." Jessica's fingers went to her lips. "Or, I'm sorry, was it cow shit?"

That was it. Matthew raised his voice above the din. "Jonas, the foul language your granddaughter has become accustomed to using, I'm sure you..."

Ready to revel in the wrath of Jonas McCabe, Matthew found himself hauled on to the dance floor.

"Does an important judge like you do this sort a thing?" Jessica played ignorant, coyly working the bantering in her favor.

But she was left speechless, as to the rhythm of the latest song, Matthew began to twirl her effortlessly. Jessica's amazement at his ability to "cut a rug", as his maternal grandfather used to say, was hard to miss.

Unexpectedly the tempo slowed. A soft melody filled the air, and Matthew lost himself in the woman and why he'd been drawn to the dance.

The music surrounded, and all he knew was the warmth of Jessica's body and her gentle grasp in his open palm.

She held his gaze defiantly. Eyes, a lightening blue, he realized instantly would eternally be a part of him.

Jessica blushed. "The song has ended, Judge."

They were standing alone on the deserted dance floor. The band had exited the stage for a break.

She excused herself from his encircling arms.

The sound of the old truck engine ricocheted off the bluff into the darkness. The faithful Chevy in gear, Matthew tried to drive away from the memories.

***

Jessica stood at the bedroom window. She couldn't sleep. "Way to be in control, McCabe." Her sarcastic scolding filled the bedroom. "The only person who could possibly be more upset about tonight is you." Jessica, looking skyward, could all too clearly imagine her grandfather reeling.

Haven't you learned by now? Never trust a Cassidy.

Jessica crawled into bed. Under her grandmother's handmade quilt, she picked up the book from the nightstand.

Riveting her eyes to the page, Jessica concentrated. But the words quickly faded and she was lured out the window to the dark October sky and a place she seldom went.

She had been at the campus library that night. Being an

animal science major meant living at the library during midterms.

Attempting to focus on her studies, she was repeatedly distracted by the person behind her tapping their pencil. Adding to the irritation, no sense of rhythm.

Finally hitting the limit, Jessica had spun around to put an end to the "pencil" recital.

Glancing up from his studies, Matthew Cassidy's pencil stopped in mid tap. Serving an internship at a local law firm, he was there doing research for a case.

She had known Matthew Cassidy her whole life. The antagonistic relationship had proved for both entertaining from an early age. But she had not seen him much since the summer of her junior year when they had shared a dance at the county fair.

The friction between the Cassidy and McCabe families was indisputable. An explanation as to what had happened Jessica had never really gotten. Nevertheless, over the years it had become quite clear, the arrogance and loathing Joseph Cassidy directed at Jonas was due to his fight for the independent farmer. The Cassidy's never-ending purchase of farmland around the county proved to be quite the opposite. The fact the Cassidy and McCabe acreages were adjacent to each other contributed to many interesting encounters.

Despite the long-standing feud, they had gone for coffee that night, talking into the wee hours. The friendship seemed predestined.

Then came the final day of classes before Christmas break. Jessica had decided to go out and celebrate with friends, arriving at the dorm late that night to discover she was locked out, her key inside.

Pounding for what seemed an eternity, she gave up. Most students had left for the holiday. Getting colder by the minute, Jessica decided to walk to Matthew's apartment, hoping he was there.

Matthew had just finished locking the front door when he saw her. Finding her snow-laden body quite humorous, he invited Jessica inside.

Needless to say, she was chilled to the bone. Matthew had started a fire and coffee as she stripped out of her wet jeans and shirt. He was adjusting some kindling when she came into the room.

Jessica had slipped on one of his flannel shirts and found herself lost in the smell of it. It hung to just above the knees, while the sides slanted up, ending a few inches below her hip. She had discovered some wool socks in a drawer.

"I hope it's okay if I borrow these until my clothes are dry?" Jessica knew she should feel embarrassed. Instead, she was taken in by the way he looked at her.

Matthew nodded, moving his focus to the fire. The deep gulp of air noted.

As the snow swirled and sparkled outside the window, the two friends became enraptured with each other's company. On the loveseat, facing the fire, Jessica's uncontrollable shaking prompted Matthew to move some pillows onto the floor closer to the heat. Grabbing a blanket from his room, they watched the flames.

Reaching forward to cover her feet, she had not anticipated the proximity to Matthew. As he turned from adjusting the fire, their lips, without any forethought, touched.

"I wonder if my clothes are dry yet?" Jessica quickly stood up and headed to the laundry room across the hall.

The frigid air of the hallway relieved the hot crimson rush. The clothes still damp, she started the dryer again, taking a few minutes to compose herself.

"Hungry?" Matthew's inquiry came from the small kitchen as she closed the apartment door. "Some soup will help sober you up."

Jessica's temper flared at the insinuation. Any attempt to hide her drunken state had failed. "Matthew I am not drunk!" She dropped in front of the fire.

He entered the room balancing two bowls. Steam rolled, and rich tempting aroma drifted through the air.

Her stomach rumbled.

The tension of the previous exchange eased.

He set the bowl on the floor in front of her. "Okay...whatever you say." The smirk matched the condescending voice perfectly.

It struck a chord and served to infuriate Jessica. "Matthew Cassidy, I am nooot dr..unk..." her declaration, somewhat slurred, angered her more. "Don't look at me like that you --"

"I'm sorry, Jess."

Perhaps she had overreacted. He meant nothing.

"And don't worry. It happens to every good little Iowa

farm girl fresh off the farm in the big city." Matthew, against the couch, hands behind his head was clearly quite proud of his flawless delivery.

The fire popped and cracked, applauding his achievement.

Jessica straddled him, so close his breath warmed her cheeks. She fell into his eyes as she had the night of the dance. Only this time she did not stop there as auburn hair cascaded around them.

"I'm not that little girl anymore, Matthew."

Before he could respond, she exited the room in defiant triumph.

Matthew came up behind her as she pulled her clothes from the dryer.

Determined to keep the upper hand, she faced him.

"You can't go out this way, Jess."

He was right. She hated it, but he was right. Besides, where would she go?

"Truce?"

His "Scouts' Honor salute" defeated her resolve.

"Good. Now while we let these get a little drier we'll have some coffee." He put the clothes in the machine.

Jessica remembered returning to the apartment, crawling onto the loveseat and covering up with a blanket. The fire danced, coaxing her to sleep.

The sizzling resonated in Jessica's head. Her nose identified the scent. She cautiously opened one eye to the morning light piercing the edge of the curtain. Her mind registered bacon, eggs and coffee.

Jumping from the loveseat, she ran to the bathroom, a movement her body was not prepared for. Bracing for the worst against the cool porcelain sink, the nausea diminished. The mirror told Jessica it would be in everyone's best interest if she freshened up.

A short while later, showered, she entered the kitchen.

Matthew greeted Jessica with a plate heaping with eggs, bacon and pancakes.

"I...wow, this is great, but I--"

"Eat it." He placed a mug in front of her and filled it to the top. "You'll be better off."

She was too tired to argue.

An awkward tension hung as Matthew drove Jessica to the dorm. She swore they were hitting every red light. Getting home to the farm could not come any too soon.

A few hours had passed as she descended the dormitory stairwell to the entrance. Stepping into the bright winter day, she saw his truck parked next to her tried-but-true-Chevy.

He sat on the tailgate of the pickup, staring up at the sky, heavy with the promise of snow.

Angry for going too far the night before, and scared by how much she wanted to do it again, Jessica tried to seem as unaffected as possible.

"I'm sorry, sir, but there are no more drunken damsels in distress here today." Walking around to the trunk, slightly ajar from the previous load, she nudged it and slid the boxes filled with books inside.

His silence was unnerving.

She slammed the trunk lid and faced the driver's side where Matthew now stood.

"Jess, I want you to know...we..."

Her skin tingled with humiliation. She had been such an idiot. He thought of her as a friend, and she had crossed the line. It would be impossible to go back.

"Matthew, I was drunk. You were right, the little McCabe girl had more than enough to drink, was a complete idiot, and I'm sorry for--"

Jessica's self-incrimination stopped short as Matthew began to softly kiss her.

At first, she resisted, pushing him away.

Then he said the words that transformed her world.

She blinked furiously as the stars blurred in the night sky outside her window. There truly was a fine line between love and hate.

CHAPTER 9

Monday morning always felt like Monday morning no matter what country Steven Conrad woke up in. He assimilated it to the color blue. Gracier, Iowa had an especially blue cast to it today.

He looked up at the crack in the plaster above his head. The eight year-old boy, with the ever-inquisitive mind had followed its twisting, turning pattern, imagining the great weaving Amazon River. As a teenager, the unsure path he sometimes wanted to take. And now as a seasoned world traveler the simple, familiar crack in the plaster brought much needed peace.

Steven could hear his mother bustling in the kitchen below. Whenever he pictured his mother, it was in an apron. Seeing her without one seemed almost unnatural.

His father was commenting on a story in the paper. Coffee and the morning paper, his father's ritual. Nothing was steadier than Arthur Conrad, Gracier's Postmaster for a quarter century. Perhaps that's what gave Steven the confidence to do the irrational. Home, always there, solid and secure.

"Steven Arthur Conrad!"

Hearing his mother's proverbial early morning warning to rise and shine, Steven unconsciously rolled his eyes then smiled at his adolescent reaction.

"No breakfast for me, Mom." This comment alone could send her into a tizzy. Adding the ultimate insult to injury when it came to his mother's obsession with homemade meals, he took it a step further. "Unless, do you have any Pop Tarts?"

You could have heard a pin drop.

Wanting to head off any panic, the possibility of it spiraling out of control, Steven jogged down the stairs ending up beside his flustered mother. "Patty Ann, I do believe you've out done yourself."

His six foot five stance dominated the pudgy, rosy-cheeked woman who pretended to swat him with her spatula.

"Hey Dad," Steven flopped into his seat at the table, "what's new in the world today?"

Art Conrad, not missing a beat between sipping his coffee and reading, peered over the top of the paper at his son. "You know better than I, and more than I would want to." He folded the paper and placed it on the table. "How's Jess?"

Steven wondered if his father perceived the change in his son at the mention of her name. It was hard to keep up the act around Art.

"She held up pretty well at the funeral."

A stack of pancakes and two crisp pieces of bacon were deposited in front of the senior Conrad.

"Thank you, Mrs. Conrad." Picking up his fork with one hand, Steven's father skillfully doused his breakfast with syrup using the other.

The man defied convention, having consumed many a high calorie, high cholesterol breakfast, he remained trim and in perfect health.

"Patty Ann Pancakes!" Steven laid it on thick for his mother, licking his lips while rubbing his hands together in exaggerated, anxious, anticipation. She pretended to be irritated, but he had witnessed her reflection in the stainless steel stovetop too many times to buy the act.

"We hadn't even finished drying the dishes from the funeral dinner, and she was out the door." Patty Ann Conrad placed a heaping plate of pancakes between them.

She checked the table, sure everything was "just so" for the Conrad men, topped off her cup and took her post against the counter. "She and Joseph Cassidy seemed to have an interesting chat."

Steven saw "the look" briefly cross his father's face. Both men had been down this path with Mrs. Conrad. She was fishing. Neither one was any too anxious to wade in and take the bait.

"In fact, I heard she was rather short with him."

Steven knew Patty Ann's eyes were fixed on him. He had two choices, play stupid, which would be true, he hadn't heard anything, or ignore the comment altogether.

"I'm wrapping up my latest piece while I'm here, then

taking some vacation." This statement would either throw his mother for a loop, as he hadn't taken more than a couple days off during the holidays since he'd been at the magazine, or it would ruffle some feathers in its blatant attempt to avoid her inquisition.

She was thrown for a loop.

"Having you around would be a big help. Your mother has quite the projects lined up for me this fall."

Steven hid the appreciative grin.

"If you're up to it we could tackle a few things this week."

He could contain it no longer. Mouth full of Patty Ann cakes, the gratitude broke through. *Way to go, Art!* Steven's unspoken praise registered quite clearly with his father.

"First is the fence."

Both men feigned shock at the instant "honey do" response.

Patty Ann plucked a long slip of paper from under a 4-H magnet on the side of the fridge. "I'll double check the list though."

The Conrad men looked intently at their plates...sweet success.

Finishing breakfast without any other close calls, Steven decided a visit uptown to Cooper's Grocery was in order. Owned by the same family for three generations, it was a mainstay in this small community.

He had worked at the store throughout high school and during college when home on break. The Coopers called him an "adopted son," and he looked forward to their company.

"Do you carry pistachios, Ma'am?" Steven having snuck up behind Adrienne Cooper whispered his request an inch from her ear.

The matriarch of the Cooper clan, six to be exact, whirled, off balance, landing in Steven's arms. The resulting partnership appeared as if they had just tangoed.

"Wow, pistachios really get people excited around here."

Adrienne Cooper wrapped her strong German arms around Steven's tall lanky frame, hugging him until no air existed in his lungs.

"You're as ornery as you are tall." Turning towards the stairs at the rear of the store she hollered, "Raymond, come see who's here!"

The store was a throwback to the simple, uncomplicated. Hard to come by in his line of work. This store, these people filled a need. He ended up here whenever he came home.

Taking him by the elbow, they walked past the staircase to the backroom and were met by the German cuss himself.

Raymond Cooper towered above most, a block of a man, a bit gruff at first, hid a heart of gold.

"Steven!"

The large paw showed years of hard work and determination. Its grasp could take you to your knees.

Raymond Cooper put his other arm around Steven. "John just went out with deliveries." He pointed at a chair next to the table that had long served as a break room amongst the inventory.

John Cooper or "Coop" to most had been one of Steven's best friends growing up. The eldest son had worked in his parents' store since the ripe old age of seven, stocking and sweeping. And he knew, even when he went to college, his true calling in life, to be in the grocery store business like the Coopers before him.

He was married, having met his wife Kristine after she moved to Gracier to be the new Kindergarten teacher. They had quite a start on the newest Cooper generation with three children currently occupying their nest and number four on the way. Steven had admired his commitment to the business and family.

"Are you sure that's what he's up to?" Steven raised an eyebrow in mock suspicion. "I used to work around that guy a lot..." For effect, he leaned in, in an apparent attempt to disclose a long hidden family secret. "I'd keep a close eye on him if I were you."

Not missing a beat, the old German grocer responded. "We've employed a few questionable characters in our day." He nodded at his wife as she placed cups for hot coffee in front of the trio. "Wouldn't you say, Mrs. Cooper?"

The familiar "ching-ring" rang out signaling a patron.

"Excuse me, Steven." Adrienne Cooper scurried out.

Raymond rose from his chair and filled each of the cups. "You in town for a while or --"

A loud thud followed by Adrienne's shout for help interrupted the two men. The sound was a familiar one to Steven. Someone had tried unsuccessfully to get something off a high shelf.

He was right behind Raymond Cooper as they came upon the source of the commotion.

"Are you alright, Samantha?"

The "floury" victim's laughter did little to alleviate the concern on the stout German face.

The young woman began brushing off the flour.

"She didn't want me climbing up there." Adrienne shook her head reprimanding the petite ghostly figure. "I told her I had two able bodies in the back."

The falling white revealed short, coal black hair. "I lift stuff heavier than that all day at the bakery, though I'm much more coordinated there." Her gaze came to rest on Steven.

"Hey Steven." A grip, strong and firm, defied the petite build.

"I'm sorry." Curious, he couldn't quite put his finger on it. But, he felt surprisingly at ease. "I'm not good at putting a face with a name, unless it's in the headlines."

"How about 'Big Bad Conrad'." Her eyes met his with a mutual recognition.

"Go and tell Caldwell?" The revelation of the flour-covered beauty's identity caught him by surprise. The last memory he had of Samantha, or Sam Caldwell, was the pig tailed little girl who tagged along, no matter how directly told, to "get lost".

"Clever as ever, eh Steven?"

Steven righted himself.

Adrienne Cooper bustled up the aisle armed with a rag, broom and dustpan. "Here dear, go outside and clean yourself up. I'll sweep this and Steven will get another bag and follow you over to the bakery." In line with Adrienne's usual fretting nature, a frown alighted. A caring hand lingered on Sam's as she gave her the rag. "I realize you want to do it all on your own, but--"

"Next time I'll call ahead, and Raymond can handle the heavy lifting." Sam's appreciation lessened the sting of the interruption. The message nonetheless, quite clear, she wanted no sympathy.

Steven noted the old grocer was impressed with the independent woman.

"Why the hell one of those boys can't see fit to date you is beyond me."

Samantha Caldwell didn't respond to Raymond Cooper's obvious exasperation with his sons' lack of pursuit, and instead chose to leave.

Pink blazed through the powdery attire, illuminating Sam's embarrassment at Raymond Cooper's comment. Outside the store's front window, she finished brushing herself off.

Grabbing the sack of flour, well above a normal person's reach, Steven hefted it onto his shoulder. "The more things change the more things stay the same." He shifted the flour for better balance. "Anything else I can get for you while I'm out, Mr. Cooper?" Steven drew on a young man from years past.

"Some common sense and a fifth of whiskey," Raymond's voice boomed from where he was retrieving flour to re-supply the shelf.

As Steven stepped out into the bright October day, Samantha Caldwell's outstretched hands met him.

"I can take it from here."

She was not happy with his offer to help, still the girl with the "do as I damn well please" attitude. He was going to have some fun with this.

"I'll get in trouble if I don't follow orders, ma'am. "Besides," he tossed a smug grin over his shoulder, "I'm bigger than you." With that, he strode down the sidewalk to the bakery.

***

Like Cooper's Grocery, the bakery was an integral part of Gracier's downtown.

Samantha Caldwell, demonstrating complete annoyance at his imposed assistance, opened the shop door wide for Steven.

Although early, the bakery was already filling up with its regular patrons. An interesting group Steven well remembered. Crows on a fence line perched to observe.

They would come to roost at the bakery in the morning. By lunchtime, the brood alighted at Hannah's. The afternoon sun would find the flock at the local coffee shop reviewing the day's news and events.

Doctors and farmers, ministers and the local barber, the mix was a cross section of Gracier folk who were in-the-know whether you wanted them to be or not.

Her body went rigid, the tension quite visible. Small town gossip required little encouragement. The glances upon his unexpected arrival were impossible to miss.

Samantha went behind the counter in a beeline for the backroom. Her effort to hasten his entrance, stopped dead in its tracks, as many life-long hometown folks shouted out a host of greetings.

"Doing my part to insure you get fresh baked goods." Steven smirked. She was not amused. The independent streak had apparently followed Sam Caldwell into adulthood.

"Steven, however will I repay you?"

Sugar sweet as he set the flour on the counter, sarcasm alighted divulging her true intent.

"No problem...I'll send you my usual fee."

"Little boys don't grow up, they just get bigger."

He stopped and turned. The flour having settled, he stared at a woman that would make any red blooded male look twice. "I don't tend to pick on little girls anymore." He fought a grin. "Now big girls, that's another story."

"Well aren't you the funny one." She started clearing and wiping the kitchen's work areas.

Steven had intended on leaving, but he found himself watching her. "Hey, where are the folks? Vacation?"

The oversized metal cookie sheet she'd been lifting onto a top rack crashed to the ground. Steven knelt to pick it up amused by Sam's current run of clumsiness.

"Dad and Mom were killed six months ago in a car wreck." Pan in hand, she climbed up on the stool, placed it on the rack and jumped back down to the floor. Spinning on her heel, she headed towards the refrigeration unit.

Steven's hand on her arm stopped Sam dead in her tracks.

"Sam, I...I'm so sorry."

She shrugged, uneasy with the attention.

"Mom usually keeps me up on...I had no idea."

Her tentative yet appreciative smile did not ease the awkwardness. His cocky attitude was gone.

"Don't worry about it." She walked to the refrigerator.

Steven fumbled, "How long had you been working in the shop with them?"

"I hadn't been." Sam slammed the freezer. "I was in Chicago, at a brokerage firm."

Then as if hearing his thoughts, Sam stopped and slid up onto the counter. The girl he once considered little more than an irritation, vanished.

"They'd been in Sioux City, visiting Michael."

Mike Caldwell was a childhood friend of Steven's, but they had lost touch. His little sister, Samantha, had been the "uninvited shadow".

"Dad told Michael he was tired, busy week, and wanted to get home." She stared out the window. "They were about 10 miles outside of town when the car left the road. The doctors believe he suffered a stroke. Dad didn't survive the crash. Mom never really came to." Her voice faded briefly. "We all got there before she passed away."

Sam scooted from the counter to face the morning sunlight appearing drawn to it.

"They all wanted to close the shop. And at first I agreed." She looked at Steven. "Most people can't wait to move out of their own personal 'one-horse town'. And I was definitely gone." The glow of the day's promise again lured Sam into the sun's radiance.

"I came here to pack up the shop and I came across those."

Steven followed her finger pointing to at least a dozen yellowed scraps of paper pinned neatly on a bulletin board. Some were recipes and some were notes all written by Sam's parents, their signatures scribbled at the bottom.

"After reading them I knew I wasn't going back to Chicago." Sam picked up a towel lying on the counter.

The sun, dancing across the top of Sam's raven black hair, cast a halo. Steven couldn't take his eyes off her.

"Sorry, probably more than you expected to hear." She hung the towel up next to the work area. "I better check on the gang out front."

She left before Steven could stop her, and was immediately met by many a "curious crow" to say the least.

Good Lord, do these people have nothing better to do? Gracier's very own press corp. Although Steven wagered they were a lot tougher.

"We started another pot for you, Sam." Hannah Johnston, owner and head cook of the town's favorite diner, behind Sam's counter, waved hello.

Steven caught Hannah's not so subtle assessment.

"What would I do without you, Ms. Johnston?" Sam cleared the latest round of cups from the counter. The tingling began to travel. *Damn! Why should I be embarrassed? Life in a fishbowl.*

"I'll grab my baked goods for the day and be on my way." Hannah patted her hand. Unwarranted, the café owner, like a mother hen, kept Sam under a protective wing.

"Oh, and honey," Hannah touched each finger of her right hand to her thumb, "I'll need four, no, five dozen cinnamon rolls tomorrow. I'm doing chili, and the boys love your cinnamon rolls with my chili." She winked at Steven standing in the kitchen doorway.

"Steven...you be sure to be there." Hannah grabbed the boxes filled with her order. "I'll be expecting you...it's still your favorite I assume?" The bakery door's bells chimed a farewell.

All eyes came to rest on Sam and her unscheduled guest. A full force inquiry was bound to hit. None was any too shy.

"If you wouldn't mind taking this to Adrienne." Sam tossed the towel.

Catching it, Steven Conrad obliged the not too subtle hint to leave.

"Thanks again, and tell the Coopers I'll be there after lunch to pick up the rest of my order." She did an about face and headed towards the jury. "Refills comin' up."

CHAPTER 10

The 1957 Cadillac Eldorado rolled up the lane, its upswept fins glistening in the morning sun. Spotless, you could eat off the car's hood.

Andrew had insisted on picking her up for the reading today. She chalked it up to his need to take care of her.

He pushed the car door wide as she approached. "Morning, Hon."

"Doctor, I believe you run the risk of polishing the paint right off this automobile." Jessica's comment, mimicking her grandfather, was ignored. Nevertheless, to not tease him about the shine on the beautifully maintained Eldorado would have served as an insult.

Putting the classic car into gear, he drove down the lane.

Andrew turned south, driving the "long way" into town.

"Aren't we going to be late?"

He stared out over the hood of the car.

"Andrew?"

"Jessica, before we get to the attorney's office I think we

better talk about a few things."

The good doctor, protective as always, but this was a little overboard.

"Andrew, I'll be fi--"

"There will be some people here today you may not be expecting."

The hairs on the back of Jessica's neck rose. Gut instinct fired, its effects smoldered inside her.

Andrew didn't take his eyes from the road.

"Okay, Doctor." Something was up. Jessica knew the tone. Her grandfather had mastered it. The good doctor had taken note. "Andrew," she chose her words carefully, "don't let me go in there unprepared."

They were no more than a few blocks away from George Reynolds' office, Jonas' attorney.

"Honey, some of the things that will be discussed today..."

His hands gripped the wheel. The pit in Jessica grew tighter.

"Matthew will be there."

Jessica couldn't breathe as shock and anger battling for control drew her chest tight. "What in the hell?" Anger had won. "Oh my God, he's contesting the will isn't he?" The grip she had on the handle tightened. "Andrew what--"

"No, no he's not contesting."

He was struggling. Things were going to get much worse. Her mind raced as they pulled up in front of the Reynolds Law Firm.

Andrew put his hand on her white knuckled fist. "I can't

tell you anymore, partly because of the promise to your grandfather."

Jessica met his gaze. There was the same deep sadness and confusion.

"And honey, mostly because I don't know." He got out and walked around the Cadillac.

Her first instinct, storm into the office and demand to know what was going on, but she knew better, if only for the moment. Steeling herself, she stepped out.

As a doctor's office distinguished itself by the intrusion of antiseptic, there was also a defined smell attributed to an attorney's office. Jessica's nostrils filled with the intense aroma of books and leather as they entered.

Her eyes darted around the reception area like a caged animal ready to spring. *What in the world was happening? Jessica's mind was a blur. And why?*

She could not trust Matthew and his supposed "good intentions." *Again the fool.*

The doors to George Reynolds' office ajar, Jessica could see people seated in stuffed leather chairs inside the wood paneled room.

George had always handled Jonas's legal business. Tall and gangly, with a humble, no frills way about him, he was Gracier's very own Jimmy Stewart.

Stepping out of his office, he crossed the foyer.

"Why, why...hello Jessi," he spoke in his halted, careful manner.

His hands encircled her grasp.

"It's been much too long. I...I wish it were under happier

circumstances."

She hugged him, then, kissed his time-etched face. "George, what am I being led into here?"

George, his arm around Jessica, escorted her to a small conference room at the end of the hall.

Andrew chose to wait outside.

"Jessi, confidentiality keeps me from...from telling you anything prior to the reading." He leaned against the table that filled the room as she moved to one of the high back leather chairs. "Except for this..."

Jessica could tell he was gauging himself.

"Today you will learn about some things your grandfather did to ensure you were...are taken care of." The seasoned attorney was struggling. "And at first it may not seem that way, but your grandfather had a reason for everything...*everything* he did."

Her legs trembled uncontrollably. Steadying herself, she followed the hall to his office.

Stepping inside, she recognized Chester's gray balding head, his unspoken greeting, one of sympathy. Or perhaps guilt? *Two older gentlemen were going to have a lot of explaining to do.*

Glancing in the opposite direction, she froze. Matthew Cassidy, in a chair, to the right of the doorway.

Andrew, moving up behind Jessica, accompanied her to the two chairs sitting left of George Reynolds' large dark walnut desk.

Treading, just above panic level, Jessica stopped short of gasping out loud.

George Reynolds, attorney for the deceased, began to speak, "This is the reading of the Last Will and...and Testament of Jonas A. McCabe."

The attorney's mouth was moving, she could hear him, but all fell into a void.

She willed herself to look composed, reserved, no hint of confusion. He would not get the satisfaction.

"As partner in the Lancaster County Land Corporation, I hereby bequeath my percentage of ownership including all rights and privileges to my sole heir, Jessica McCabe." George allowed the information to sit there.

What was that look? Panic surged.

It then rolled off George's tongue, "A meeting of the parties involved in said Corporation, including my named heir, shall...shall convene following this reading to review with said heir the responsibilities of ownership in the Corporation."

Partners? The epiphany struck. *Oh Dear God!*

She imagined the smug expression and refused to turn in his direction.

Jessica could see him shift. *Was he uneasy? Or getting a better look at the woman he had fooled once again?*

Questions that filled her mind went from Jonas to Andrew. *What could he have possibly said or done to win their trust?* This was a bad dream, a horrible nightmare. *Hold on.* Maybe she had assumed too much.

"Excuse me, George," Jessica cut the tension filling the attorney's office. "Are all the people in this room partners in the corporation?"

George Reynolds lowered the document he was reading, but showed no sign of straying off the course set forth for him by Jonas McCabe.

The well-mannered attorney removed the black reading glasses perched half way down his nose. "It is a corporation Jonas and several other individuals formed." Settling the spectacles on his nose, he adjusted their placement, shifted the papers and accessed his progression.

His methodical movements were getting on her extremely raw nerves. He was stalling.

"As directed by your grandfather, a meeting will occur following this reading to clear up any questions you may...may have, Jessica."

Jessica wasn't about to sit patiently. "George--"

Andrew tapped her arm.

A little girl acknowledged the silent suggestion. *Behave.* She conceded to the instruction of her elder. "I'm sorry, continue."

The remainder of the reading contained bequests to St. John's, the local school and other organizations Jonas had been involved in, all things Jessica had fully expected.

George, glasses off, placed the will on the desk and folded his hands. The reading was finished.

"This has been a surprise to some of you, and there are questions to be...answered. So, as per Jonas' will, I recommend we proceed. With the majority of partners present, I call this meeting to order." George glanced around the room. "I suggest we...we move to the conference room." Coming from behind his desk, he gestured for the group to follow.

Jessica didn't move, unsure if her legs would hold up. *Keep your composure, McCabe.*

"Jessica." Andrew brought her abruptly back to the room. "I won't ask if you're okay, I know better."

Could he sense the bewilderment, the feeling of betrayal?

"Let's go get some answers."

The group had just settled in around the oval table when the door swung.

"Sorry I'm late." Mickey Hansen burst into the room. "Damn beer man was late, and..." the local bar owner took in the group surrounding the table.

"We're glad you're here." George pointed at the seat beside Jessica. "Now we can maybe explain a few things to this young lady." George Reynolds seemed to be mulling over in his mind how to begin when Mickey, in his usual no frills manner, spoke up.

"Jessi," he moved forward, elbows on his knees and looked directly into her eyes, "you remember when the bank began foreclosing on quite a few farms around here?"

She nodded.

"Well, those families had been put in a position by the bank and its board where, barring a miracle, there was no way they could financially survive." The heavy dose of animosity at the mention of the local institution was undeniable.

"Some board members, who shall remain nameless, involved in some questionable transactions had all but clinched a deal. The land would be foreclosed on and sold to the highest bidder."

Jessica knew full well who was on the bank board and who that highest bidder had been, which made Matthew's presence even more confusing.

"Well, Jonas and a couple other wise old men," he motioned in the direction of Andrew and Chester, "they had an idea. They approached a few others in the local community and put together a corporation made up of "silent partners." Mickey appeared to seek George's approval. "Anyway, this secret band of Merry Men...well, we *procured* from the greedy and gave to those who deserved it."

Jessica observed the partners as they waited, wondering who would speak up next. They seemed cognizant to the fact that up until now, Jonas had only disclosed two of the corporation's partners to Jessica.

"Jessica," Andrew's voice was calm and low. One she imagined he used when at someone's bedside.

Jessica looked to Andrew.

Mickey tilted back in his chair, relief that someone had taken up where he had left off quite apparent.

"If the landowners had discovered everyone behind this corporation...well there are some very proud, head strong people who worked this land for years and friendship or not, they would not have taken kindly to it." Andrew shook his head. "They are not people who take handouts."

Stubborn Iowa pride, it grew as thick as corn and like the golden harvest, in good supply. Jessica was blessed with more than her fair share.

"And secondly, if anyone on the Lancaster County Bank Board ever found out who certain corporation members were," Andrew fought a smirk, "well, it goes without saying, some feathers would have been more than ruffled."

Jessi's gaze went over Dr. Andrew Harrison's shoulder.

Matthew pushed back his chair and walked to the far end of the room.

Jessica suppressed the urge to scream, to use every foul profanity she'd been told never to use. Instead, in this nightmare, this terrible, gut-wrenching nightmare, he stood before a bookcase covering one entire wall of the conference room.

"My father and I share an office." Matthew paused. "We are far from sharing a similar point of view."

His father. Joseph Cassidy, chairman of the bank board and although never proven, the driving force behind the plan to take the land out from under a group of unsuspecting farmers.

She could still picture the anger bright in Jonas' eyes the day he had told her.

"I learned about the land deal before it became public." He stood against the backdrop of the floor to ceiling bookshelves.

"You're thinking Joseph Cassidy's son has no business being here. You're right."

His bluntness set off knowing glances around the table.

"But I didn't ask to be here, Jess. Jonas approached me." She hated that smile.

"And I was more than willing to help him with his

project."

There had to be more to this than anyone was letting on. She knew she'd get more out of them one on one. *Divide and conquer.* It had worked her whole life. However, this situation went far beyond child's play.

"Jonas knew you would want...want answers, Jess." George moved to Jessica. "He gave me this."

George placed a key on the conference room table. She recognized it as a key to a lock box.

Jessica reached for the key, its cool metal a shock to her trembling fingers. *Like a step off the cliff in those childhood dreams.* A jolt, passing the veil of sleep into what is real. Jessica gasping from dark subconscious into the light of reality, to the world she knew to be true and safe.

She peered out to her lights of hope. They were not bright, but dim. Very dim. The shadow of concern cast full circle.

Jessica's attempt to appear okay failed. They were part of this entire nightmare.

"What will I find, George?" Fear overtook at the uncertainty she met.

"I'm...I'm not sure." George sat down. "He usually left the key with me, so you would receive it at...at the appropriate time. But once in a while he would come by the office and take it with him...for a couple days, the last being a few days after we finalized the paperwork on...on the Land Corporation."

Jessica stood. "If you all don't mind, I need a few minutes." She had to get out of this room now. "George, can

I use your office please?"

The Gracier noon whistle blew.

Chester took its cue. "Why don't we order some food from Hannah's and while we wait, Jess can have a moment to herself."

George Reynolds accompanied Jessica to his office. "You take your...your time." He motioned to a wingback chair. "Maxine will...will bring you something to drink. Coffee? A pop?"

"A diet whatever you have would be fine."

He left the room.

Maxine entered with a Diet Pepsi. "Honey, you need anything else..." She patted her arm gently.

Jessica looked at the key and then out the window behind George Reynolds' desk. The clock on the side of the bank showed 12:15.

***

"Excuse me, gentlemen." George Reynolds' secretary crossed the room quietly and spoke into the attorney's ear.

He nodded and thanked her as she exited the room.

"Jessica told Maxine she had to...to take care of something." He sighed heavily. "She's left."

"Damn."

Andrew's response signaled to Matthew, the doctor knew exactly where she was going. The sick knot, in Matthew's stomach since Jessica arrived for the reading, ascended to his throat.

"I'm coming with you, Andrew. She can't--"

"I'm going alone, Matthew." Doctor Andrew Harrison

shut the door behind him.

Matthew studied the confusion relaying around the room trying to catch any hint, any clue. *Did they know? Did any of them know?*

Mickey Hansen's bluntness cut to the chase. "What the hell is in that lock box?"

CHAPTER 11

The Lancaster County Bank bustled with activity as customers went about lunchtime errands. Jessica handed the teller behind the lock box counter the key.

"*We* have to do this."

Drained from the morning's events, she had no comeback for the good doctor. He had found her. And that said enough.

"I'll call a bank officer to assist with the box inventory." The bank teller indicated the lines the two executors were required to sign.

Procedure, yes, but she had had more than her fill of playing by the rules today.

Retrieving the oversized box from the vault, Jessica and Andrew were led to the bank's conference room and seated at its dark oak table.

Jessica began to shake. She clenched her hands in her lap, hoping to hide the physical reaction of raw, tired nerves.

The officer lifted the lid on the metal box. Jessica's eyes

went to the deep expanse.

Slowly, methodically, the bank officer withdrew each item, documenting it on a bank form. The pace bordered on excruciating.

She wasn't sure what she had expected to see. But as the metal bank box was emptied, she became acutely mindful of how meticulously her grandfather had organized its contents. Sealed manila and business envelopes soon filled the table. A half hour had passed until finally the entire safe deposit box was empty.

Andrew scanned the table, resolute. The confirmation of betrayal overwhelmed her. She had a sneaking suspicion Andrew was following Jonas McCabe's strict instructions.

Using the box the officer had provided, Andrew placed each item in it.

The bank officer slid the forms across the table for Andrew and Jessica to sign. Thanking him for his assistance, they walked out of the bank.

***

They entered the farmhouse neither saying a word.

Andrew went to the cupboard and started the coffee.

Odd perhaps.

Today however, all normalcy had flown out the window. Jessica placed the box on the kitchen table.

Andrew turned from the dark brew.

Jessica let her gaze go out the window to the Iowa countryside. The golden amber on the densely leaved trees stood in sharp contrast to the black farm fields beyond. She prayed for its rolling beauty to invade her thoughts, to close out the turmoil.

"I'm scared, Andrew." Jessica focused on the horizon, its simple true line distorted as the battle to right herself waged. "Am I ready for this?"

Andrew didn't respond but instead began laying envelopes on the table.

Cold anxious fear creeped in again.

Coming back from the world outside, Jessica assessed the various envelopes. Some had writing on them and some didn't. A copy of the will and the Lancaster Land Corporation sat to one side. Then Andrew reached for an envelope that read "pictures".

"This one first." He placed a bulky manila package in front of her.

She pinched the well-worn metal clasps and opened the flap. Jessica peered inside to see a bundle of pictures. As she slid the bundle out a beautiful, smiling young woman in a graduation gown appeared. Maggie McCabe, her mother. And standing on either side, parents, Jonas and Ann McCabe, so young and proud.

Andrew watched as Jessica flipped through the photos. There were many pictures of her mother's high school days and possibly college.

Jessica stopped on the image of a young woman, pregnant, standing by the fence at the north end of the pasture.

She had never seen a photo of her pregnant mother. Tall and slender even with a child growing in her, she was beautiful. Though taken at a distance there was no mistaking

Maggie McCabe's expression, lost.

"It was rough, but your mother loved carrying you." Andrew unknowingly addressed the burden.

Had she been Maggie McCabe's biggest regret?

"She read whatever she could find on caring for a baby." He chuckled. "We had quite the discussions when she came in for check-ups."

Jessica was grateful for the unintended comfort of the story.

She continued, asking questions about some photos, while for others no explanation was necessary. Yellowed, the pictures opened up a door to the past, ajar, never to be closed. It frightened Jessica. A reaction she had not expected.

Andrew pointed to a high school yearbook. Jessica had been dumbfounded when the clerk had pulled it from the box.

"You'll see a lot of your mother in those pages Jessica."

As she flipped the pages of the picture-filled time capsule, it became evident Maggie McCabe had been a well liked girl. Grinning teenagers surrounded her in every photo.

Gradually people revealed themselves. "Andrew, is that who I think it is?" Jessica pointed at a hefty red headed fellow mugging a shot for the photographer.

"That's Mickey alright."

Jessica derived comfort from the knowledge that Mickey provided a link, as did the book.

It was a window into the past. A window she wasn't quite ready to look through. She closed the leather bound yearbook.

Andrew didn't question Jessica's decision but instead began to review each envelope, briefly explaining the contents. Some were put to the side for later.

Then Andrew withdrew a letter, unlike the crisp well-ordered envelopes before. He took on a hushed, almost reverent tone, "Even though this is worn, the only one who ever looked inside the pages was your grandfather."

Jessica became transfixed on the yellow dog-eared envelope he held in his hand. She was sure Andrew noted her hesitation.

"Jonas wrote it for you alone. What you choose to share is up to you."

Part of her wanted to grab the letter. Part wanted never to touch it.

"I think it's best if I leave you to read this." Andrew placed it in front of her.

"On one condition," she looked up at him, "if I have questions--"

"I'll be out first thing tomorrow. Bright and early."

The back door slammed its farewell. The rumble of the Cadillac Eldorado reverberated off the corncrib.

She flipped the worn envelope. A piece of tape held it closed. It was not the first one to be affixed. She traced the tattered yellow edges. Apprehension drew her fingers away from the sealed secrets. Jessica scanned the table covered with frozen pieces of time.

The desire to make sense of the insanity had her pulling the pages from the envelope.

A sharp breath burned Jessica's lungs.

June 19, 1963
Dear Jessica,

The day after Jessica was born and her mother died.

Jessica imagined the pain and loss of a father, her grandfather.

She ran her hand across the faded ink. He had the courage to write it, she owed him no less then to read it.

Crying subsided into laughter and back again to tears at the pages containing his handwritten memories.

The first day of school to the lazy afternoons spent fishing, the pages were filled. She was amazed with all the things he had written and reflected upon. Her heart tore.

Then, he began to explain the Lancaster County Land Corporation and its most troubling partner.

> *Honey, I'm sure your mind is filled with a million questions. And if you're reading this, Jess, it means I didn't get a chance to tell you all I needed to.*
>
> *First, I'll start with the Land Partnership and how it came about.*
>
> *Matthew had gotten information about the properties to be foreclosed on, and he couldn't directly do anything about it. But he knew Andrew and I could. The rest of the partners are "silent partners". Please honor this.*

This goes against everything I have ever said about the Cassidys. You can trust him, Jess. I was wrong.

Her eyes locked on the words...*trust him.*

Now honey, about your Mom.

Jessica's throat grew thick as the sob slipped. *Mom, her Mom*, a phrase she had rarely heard let alone seen it written. Wiping away the flood of emotion, she continued to read.

I'm not sure I have it all right yet, Jess. It is why I haven't told you these things. I was wrong to keep your mother just beyond reach. I realize now it was to protect a foolish old man. Forgive me, Jess.

Jessica put the lukewarm cup of coffee to her mouth. *Oh my God, this needed to be something stiffer.*

She had decided at a young age to put the longing to know Maggie McCabe to rest. It caused Jonas too much pain. Now, like him, she faced the memories alone.

Jessica became engulfed as Jonas described her mother Maggie's short life, in intricate detail, the love for his daughter, boundless. And it was clear the letter had been written as much for Jessica's sake as it had for Jonas', to come to terms.

Your mother loved to paint. In the loft, you will find the beautiful works of art she created. They will tell you more about your mother than I ever could. The key is there.

She sat stunned. "The loft? Where in the loft?" Jessica's voice echoed off the kitchen wall. She knew every inch of that barn. Her eyes raced down the page for some explanation.

Don't be afraid, Jessica. I pray Andrew is there to help you as he did me.

My greatest hope is that before you read these pages I've found and given you what you will be seeking.

I love you my precious grandchild.

Jonas

CHAPTER 12

She'd watched her grandfather hang the keys to the loft above the doorway countless times. But never had she noticed the third key on the ring, slightly different, not as worn and smaller.

The late afternoon sun glimpsed between the buildings, spilling into the office window as she headed up the stairs. Beating in her chest like a drum, Jessica's heartbeat thudded in her ears. What did the key open? A chest? A box? *A room?*

Walking around the loft, Jessica's eyes darted, combing the walls. Then, behind a stack of dusty supply boxes, she noted the slightest deviation in the barn's wall. She shoved the stack of supplies, the weight not registering.

A small door, not much taller than Jessica revealed itself, no knob, just a padlock with a latch. The key fit perfectly. The lock popped.

The light she had seen peeked through small gaps in the barn siding. The room was dark and musty. She then saw a switch to the right.

The light flooded the little room. She blinked and squinted, adjusting to the stark white illumination. Tarps draped unfamiliar shapes against the walls of the small room. She carefully lifted the heavy fabric.

***

His mind hadn't stopped racing since the call to Andrew, the old doctor reluctant to tell Matthew anything.

What had been in that lock box? What had Jonas shared with her?

As he knocked for the second time, Matthew spied the barn loft's window and the light dangling from the ceiling.

Heading down the gravel lane to the large red building, he entered the office, took the stairs and walked across the loft towards the small, lighted doorway.

Stooping under the small entry, his vision adjusted to the light and he saw her, sitting among dozens of paintings.

The beauty and clarity of the artwork encompassed the tiny room. The work was stunning. Portraits of people, scenes of the farmland, all laid out in a spectrum of subtle brushstrokes.

"They're my mother's."

"My God Jess, they're incredible." He could see the curve of her cheek moist with tears.

He kneeled beside her. "Jess." The need to hold her, to take care of her, was overwhelming. *Damn it, this isn't right.*

But the tug of war Jonas had entrusted him to live with was not to be resolved, not here, not now. She had dealt with enough today.

"Did you know about this too, Matthew?" Distant, cold,

her intense blue eyes fixed on a painting.

"No, Jess." His mind struggled, as it always did, with Jonas' demand.

"And I should believe you?"

The drop of torment descended. Without thinking, Matthew brushed it away. Well-hidden longing coursed as his fingertips rested on her cheek.

Jessica stood up and crossed the room. "Please go, Matthew. I can't..."

To comprehend, to bear, was too much. His presence was the final straw. But he didn't move. He had to figure out what she had discovered and then determine if he could or should tell her anything.

"I'm not leaving, Jess." Matthew brushed the barn floor dirt from his knees.

"You've done it before, you can do it again."

She had every right to say it.

"He says you were the one behind saving the land." Stoic, the pain and anger contained was unmistakable. Her eyes, intense, pierced him.

How much longer could he keep it hidden? *Forever, the promise was forever.*

"He says you can give me the answers I'm looking for..." Her voice dropped to a whisper, "He says I'm to trust you."

The anguish, he had withstood it once. *Could he do it again?* "Jess, there's a lot you don't understand, I--"

"Don't understand, don't understand!"

He could not deny it anymore. Jessica's forgiveness was

unthinkable.

"You're in a land deal with my grandfather...*a Cassidy*! Everyone I care about has known. I'm given a letter from Jonas telling bits and pieces of a past, which up until now, have been all but completely hidden from me. And then this room!"

Jessica stopped. He knew she was angry with herself for losing control.

"And now you..." Jessica's entire body was shaking.

He came up next to her. "Jess, let me explain." Jonas hadn't told her. Relief clashed with fear.

"Explain what?"

The voice startled both of them.

Steven Conrad ducked through the doorframe and into the room.

"Explain nothing." Jessica held him in a defiant gaze. "He was just leaving."

Steven. Always the hero. Matthew held back. He didn't want anyone to hear what she should learn from him alone. Especially Steven Conrad.

Steven moved further into the room, leaving an obvious exit.

The all too familiar rush enfolded him as she fell into his arms.

"How did you know to come?"

Steven looked into the tear-streaked face. Eyes swollen and nose running, she still had his heart. "Doc called me."

"And his prescription?" She accepted the handkerchief.

"Only that you might want to talk."

CHAPTER 13

Sam Caldwell remembered sitting on her family's front porch as a child. It seemed huge then. In her adolescence, it became Sam's window on the world, where someday her horizons would be far away from this small town she called home, adventure and excitement calling.

She gazed out over the white porch railing, admiring the last copper colored folds of the autumn sunset, going into the world she had once dreamed would give her everything. Instead, its red and orange rays were setting on the place true contentment resided. Something that child had always known.

She set the glass filled with dark red wine on the gently worn table. It had been the spot for her father's coffee and her mother's lemonade after a full day at the shop.

Busy as they were, she loved her days at the bakery. She awakened the dark, sleepy, quiet streets of this small Iowa town. And as the sun reached into a new day, the chiming of the bakery's front door welcomed it as faithful patrons passed. Morning until early afternoon, it signaled the comings and goings of many a Gracier resident.

Some were customers she'd waited on as a child. And others, childhood friends who like Sam, whether by choice or circumstance, had ended up calling the small community home.

Sam hadn't altered much about the bakery except for some additional equipment to help her one-person operation. The recipes and the personal touch had remained the same for Caldwell's Bake Shop.

At first she'd been concerned if she could earn a living, and more importantly, if the community would embrace her. The anxiety of the unknown was short-lived.

As the months passed, she had fallen into the routine she had experienced from a very young age. With a family owned and operated business, everyone was a part of its success. It had helped Sam work through a lot.

She cherished the thought of Samuel Caldwell watching his daughter on the front porch, working on the bakery's books while drinking a favorite merlot. *Okay, some things had changed.*

It was with the final tip of the glass she saw him coming up the sidewalk with the enormous dog, leaving no question as to who was walking whom.

"I take it you don't do much dog walking in your line of work."

"Good evening, Miss Caldwell." Steven now stood at the white picket fence that bordered the Caldwell home.

How often throughout their childhood, had he raced up

the street, leaped the fence and dashed up the front porch stairs looking for her older brother Michael to come with him on an adventure. But tonight, oddly enough, he waited for permission to enter. She found it amusing.

"Come on up."

Casey, the Conrad's dog, ran ahead as he unlatched the gate and before Steven could stop him, bounded up the stairs to Sam. She rubbed the yellow lab's head as he wagged his tail furiously. "Hey Case, where's your buddy?" Art Conrad was the immense dog's usual partner on his nightly stroll. Sam could set her watch by it.

"He got the second string tonight." Steven reeled in the leash. "Sit, Casey."

The well-trained dog obeyed.

"Glass of lemonade?" Sam hesitated, unsure. "Or wine?"

"I believe I'll have what you're having."

Samantha pulled the screen door open catching it with the heel of her foot slowing its usually rapid, noisy close. She heard the porch swing creak. The squeaking rhythm that followed signaled he'd found himself quite at home.

The sensation began to overtake again. *Damn it. Arrogant, cocky and full of himself.* Why did he have this effect on her?

She turned to face the counter, avoiding where her emotions begged to travel. Hitting the edge of the kitchen sink the wine bottle exploded in her hand.

The screen door had barely slammed as he rounded the corner into the kitchen.

Drenched in red wine, standing barefoot, surrounded by

shards of glass, Sam's humiliation was complete.

"Well it's confirmed, you are quite coordinated. This is two for two since I've been back."

"Funny." The glare she shot in his direction missed its mark. His gaze was not on the wine glass she held in one hand or the top half of the shattered wine bottle in the other. Steven Conrad's full attention was on her wine soaked shirt now clinging all too tightly.

Why you... where do you get off! Defying his brazen reaction, she moved. The shard of glass sliced her heel. "Ouch!" Dropping both the wine glass and the remainder of the wine bottle, Sam grabbed her foot as blood flowed, dark as the merlot pooled on the linoleum. The explosion of glass on the floor completed the mortifying scene.

"Okay, hold on a minute."

She could hear the glass crunching under his thick-soled hiking boots. Then without hesitation, he picked her up.

Instinctively Sam's arms encircled his neck and shoulders. Her imagination escaped to a man and woman crossing a threshold. Scolding logic served to wipe it swiftly from her mind.

Crunching across the sharp, sparkling splinters, he carried her toward the kitchen table.

Suddenly he lost his footing. The muscles in his arms tensed for the unavoidable fall. She braced herself for the hard linoleum floor she would soon be meeting with her backside.

Steven sprawled on top of her, their lips almost touching as the kitchen table broke their fall.

"Thank you." Sam, pinned in place, fought the urge to laugh. "I think?"

*What was that look? S*he'd known this boy her entire life and had never seen this face.

Gaining his footing, Steven didn't speak but instead took hold of Sam's foot. The touch of his warm fingers as he explored the cut for glass had Sam frozen.

Was he angry?

"I don't see any glass." He lowered Sam's foot on to the table. "Sit there while I get what I need to clean this up."

Although it hurt, she was not about to sit by while he cleaned up her mess. Hopping off the table, Sam began picking up the pieces of broken wine bottle, tossing them into the sink.

"Okay, what about 'stay put' did you not understand?" Steven extended his hand helping her back up on the table. A full array of medical supplies including gauze, peroxide and a washcloth sat next to Sam.

Sam smiled sheepishly. The "clean up" he'd been referring to was her foot.

Sitting on the chair, he carefully placed Sam's foot on his lap.

"I get the impression you've done this before." Sam played tug of war with the awkward adolescent girl. *Oh, for the love of...stop it!*

Taking the cotton ball he had soaked with peroxide, Steven stroked around the cut, double-checking for any glass. The heat rising in her cheeks was unmistakable. She prayed he wouldn't look up.

"Let's just say I've been in some situations where this stuff came in handy." Not missing a beat, he finished examining the cut then reached for the alcohol. "Okay ma'am, this is going to smart a little."

The mischievous look sent Sam back to the infamous pranks of Steven Conrad and Michael Caldwell. It was time to wipe it from his face.

The ice-cold reality of the alcohol flowing into her cut and the resulting sting ruined the attempt. She gritted her teeth. He would not get the best of her.

"Well, aren't you still the toughest little girl in all of Gracier."

"You are enjoying this way too much." She felt ridiculous.

"Okay let's wrap this up." Steven worked with surprising expertise dressing Sam's foot in a matter of seconds. "There you are, Miss Caldwell." Steven gathered the medical supplies and left the room.

Getting up, Sam grabbed the leather sandals sitting at the back door, not wanting another mortifying episode. Looking down to slip the shoes on, her drenched blouse served a reminder, you could see quite clearly, what she was not wearing underneath.

Sam headed up the stairs as quickly as her injured foot would allow.

Returning to the kitchen, Steven carefully gathered the bigger pieces of glass and started to mop the floor. Hearing

Sam behind him, he glanced up.

Wearing t-shirt and jeans, the October moon framed her small, firm silhouette.

"Well, who would have thought I would live to see this day?"

Awkwardly aware of his adolescent gawking, he riveted his eyes to the floor, following the mop, soaking up the wine.

"It was usually me cleaning up after you and Michael."

"Oh now come on." Steven moved to one side as Sam rolled up the wine saturated rug. "We weren't that terrible."

"Fourth of July, 1975," her flash from the past carried from the laundry room, "firecrackers and exploding flour."

"That's why you looked so familiar in the store the other morning." Steven could not contain himself at the memory of the 13-year-old girl covered in flour, head to toe.

He and Michael hysterical, doubled over with their achievement until Samuel Caldwell, Michael and Sam's father, came in the bakery door greeted by his daughter, Casper the ghost.

"Funny, you didn't laugh much during your two weeks on kitchen duty at the bakery."

Sam's comment only widened his grin.

Choosing to ignore him, Sam pulled the refrigerator handle.

"Wait a minute." Steven stepped up behind her.

She turned to move ending up in his arms. His quick-witted attitude silenced.

"I better do the honors."

Sam picked up the corkscrew on the counter.

Taking it, he uncorked the bottle.

"Do you trust me to get the glasses?" She retrieved two.

They returned to the front porch.

A warm evening, the gentle breeze filled with the heady richness of an Iowa fall, intoxicating to Steven's senses.

Samantha began to curl her feet under. A gasp escaped, accompanied by a not so well hidden grimace. She placed the bandaged foot on the table between them.

"Had a tetanus shot recently?" Steven, pouring wine, looked up.

"That would be summer 1970. You and Michael decided to build a moat around your backyard fort and I discovered the lawn dart booby trap."

Steven winced. Sam screaming, her foot impaled on a lawn dart, was not a fond memory.

He handed Sam a glass of merlot and sat down in the swing facing her. "Does Michael suffer this kind of purgatory when he's around you?"

"No, his three sons manage that for me."

Steven chuckled at the penance Michael was surely experiencing.

"So how's Jess doing?"

Steven swirled the wine in his glass. "Okay." He looked out beyond the porch rail, uncomfortable discussing Jessica while sitting here with Samantha Caldwell.

"I catch myself expecting to see him, bright and early at the shop." She looked into her wine glass. "I'm going to miss debating that ornery, opinionated man."

Ornery wasn't the half of it. Jonas had left Jess in a real mess. It wasn't like him at all.

"I suppose I better call it a night." She drained her wine glass and set it on the table.

Her abruptness came out of nowhere.

"Running a bakery doesn't allow for a lot of late nights."

He quickly finished his merlot. "Are you sure you can handle putting this away, Miss Caldwell?"

Sam nodded as she walked to Casey, rubbing the dog between his ears once more. "See you later, boy."

Steven attached the dog's leash "Appreciate the hospitality." Pointing at Sam's injured foot, he frowned, doing his best to look fatherly. "Have Doc give it the once over tomorrow."

Sam picked up the empty glasses and half-empty wine bottle. "Goodnight, Steven." She went through the front screen door, letting it slam.

Steven began the walk home. *Samantha Caldwell.* As if things weren't confusing enough.

***

Sam filled the glass with merlot and corked the bottle. Outside the kitchen window, the tall, thin frame of Steven Conrad rounding the corner. A long sip raced to numb.

You're that little pig tailed girl whenever you're around him. Thank goodness Michael hadn't been here. He would have picked up on it in a minute. Did he? No. She was nothing more than "Little Sam Caldwell," a childhood friend's sister he had taken great pleasure in teasing.

Samantha knew the far off look at the mention of her name. He was still in love with Jessica McCabe and being reminded of it, even now...the wine gave little comfort.

CHAPTER 14

Andrew headed out to the farm early Wednesday morning. He knew she'd had visitors. How many, he wasn't certain.

As he pulled up the lane, he saw her sitting on the front step of the porch, her hair back, jeans and a sweater. So alone.

Putting the car in park, he shut off the engine and crossed the lawn to the step.

"Did you know about the room in the loft, Andrew?" Jessica stared ahead.

Andrew and Jonas had gone over this a hundred times.

"Andrew, if I die before telling Jessi, or worse, before I figure this out, you must help her through this."

He wouldn't mention the subject at all. Then something occurred bringing all his research out. Andrew believed one of those moments had caused Jonas' stroke.

"Why didn't he let me see the paintings, Andrew?"

Her question was one that had sparked many heated debates between the two old men. Andrew's greatest fear was that this young woman's determination would supersede any well thought out plan he and Jonas had concocted.

Andrew, deliberate, measured, stayed the course. "After your mother died your grandfather put her works in the room. Seeing them was too much for him."

He watched her out of the corner of his eye, fixed on the horizon, as if searching for some clarity to all of this.

Jonas had kept her mother just beyond reach. Now to find out how much Maggie had engulfed him had to be confusing.

"She, her memory, it...it haunted him, Andrew. Why?"

Andrew had asked the same of Jonas that night. Unfortunately, the answer had died with him.

Doc Andrew looked at the troubled young woman. "I promised to do this 'his way' if he wasn't here to do it."

With that, they went inside.

For the rest of the morning they reviewed envelopes that had been put to the side.

Andrew knew every item. He came to the folder that contained the empty manila envelope, and, for an instant, let his guard down. A petition to heaven fulfilled.

Jessica was too overwhelmed to detect.

Its contents had been the source of many sleepless nights for his friend. He said a prayer that Jonas had chosen to destroy it.

Looking up, Andrew met Jessica's confused expression.

"Jonas tried to prepare me for this..." There was nothing

he could do to make it any easier.

"This story Jessica is one with no definite ending and that, I'm afraid, you may have to live with." He stared at the hands that had healed many patients. Andrew prayed his words today would finally bring closure to the young woman.

"Andrew, I need to know this," Jessica wavered, emotions threatening sure to consume her.

His prayers heard, he had to figure out the next step.

From what he could gather, nothing here would lead her to the dark past. At the most, it would produce hours of frustration, taking her down numerous dead ends as it had her grandfather. The confirmation Jonas had searched for eluded him until the day he died.

He wasn't going to allow her to take the same path. That in mind, he began.

"Your grandparents were strong people, but when it came to your mother, the world stood still." Andrew recalled the day.

"She showed up at the door late one afternoon after the office was closed." The ache renewed as Maggie's torment looked to him, fresh, unfaded. "She was like one of my own children.

"We talked for quite a while. She had committed a great sin in the eyes of the church and her parents. Finally, I convinced her to tell Jonas and Ann. They were devastated." Andrew looked at Jessica. "But they came to terms with the pregnancy."

"Jonas never talked about this, Andrew," her voice was that of a frightened child.

"It was painful for him, Jess." He must make the case, make her believe. There would not be another life ruined.

"Maggie had dropped out of college and moved home to be with your grandparents. Your grandfather set up a studio for her in the loft. Painting brought her peace."

Although not clear, it seemed amazement accompanied Jessica's confusion.

Andrew wrestled with the best way to proceed.

"Maggie didn't date anyone special in high school. She always hung around with friends, no one in particular. When she did go on a date, it was usually one of the gang.

"At college she found another group of friends." Andrew smiled. "She had a personality you couldn't resist."

Damn it Jonas, what a hell of a thing to leave undone. The burden was now his.

"It ate at your grandparents Jess, their daughter going through this alone, maintaining her distance."

Andrew paused.

"What Jonas and Ann couldn't figure out, the one thing Maggie refused to tell, who your father was."

Her voice was barely there, "My father."

Silence seized the implication.

"You were born prematurely. Your mother's unexpected complications caused her to go into a coma..."

His faded eyes filled.

"There were your grandparents holding the granddaughter who had captured their hearts. Then, without warning, that was all they had left of the daughter they had loved more than life itself."

Jessica wrapped her arms around his shoulders.

"I didn't promise answers, Jess." Andrew's eyes rose from the papers. "But I'll do what I can." *Dear Lord, let this be enough for her.*

"Did Jonas figure out who my father was?"

Her intensity, the no nonsense style, she had inherited from her mother and grandfather.

"Andrew?"

Without hesitation he spoke, continuing to direct the fate of many lives, "No."

He couldn't register her reaction at first, frustration or sadness.

The phone rang, a reply to his prayers.

Jessica picked up the receiver of the well-worn black phone.

"Doc McCabe's."

Ever the vet's granddaughter, Jessica answered the phone as she had for years. Andrew knew she hadn't comprehended the significance.

"Yes this is she." Jessica listened attentively to the caller. "That's alright. Yes. Okay. Where's she at?"

Andrew was witness to Jonas' fondest dream coming true.

"How long has she been like this?" Jessica chewed her lip, her head down, listening. "I'm on my way, Carl." She hung the phone up, "Carl Jans' prize Angus is having trouble delivering her calf."

Andrew watched her focus shift. Doctor Jessica McCabe had taken the reins of her grandfather's practice with typical ease. Like Jonas, it was with her whole being, nothing less.

"I'm sorry, Andrew." Jessica stopped.

"We doctors know where our true dedication lies." He patted her hand resting on his shoulder. "Go, Doc."

"I'm okay, Andrew." She kissed him warmly on the cheek, "And I can always depend on you."

Andrew listened to the sound of her Jeep racing past the kitchen windows, out the lane within seconds.

He now carried the mantle of deception, sealed forever in the orderly package of lies. He planned to keep it that way.

***

Jessica turned into the lane of the Jans farm 15 minutes after the call. The familiar route, to be doing it again, was good.

Carl Jans met her at the entrance to the barn.

The sign above the door announced to everyone the pride he derived in raising prize-winning Angus cattle. The letters in black painted on white read identical to the sign that welcomed those who drove onto the neatly kept acreage.

JANS ANGUS CATTLE EST. 1914

"I'm sure glad I caught you, Doc."

It felt somewhat strange to be referred to as Jonas had over the years.

"She's been at this since early morning. About an hour ago it took a turn for the worse."

Jessica followed him through the barn entrance onto the neatly kept cement floor. She could hear the Angus before she could see her. The sound was one of pain and exhaustion.

Carl unlatched the gate.

Jessica rounded the corner. The immense blackness of the mighty animal greeted her. The shallow panting sent up red flags. The call may have come too late.

"Carl, are you the only one home?" Jessica didn't take her eyes off the animal, knowing full well with the strain the cow was under, she might kick at any moment, landing a lethal blow.

"I'll get the boys. They're in the field."

"Okay, girl." Jessica moved slowly, methodically, retrieving equipment from her bag. "You hang with me now. This little one needs a mama."

The cow's breathing was too labored.

The Jans men entered the barn. It was evident they had run all the way.

"Okay Carl, you and Clark stand here." She pointed to the cow's head. "Get a good hold on her."

Fortunately, the Angus wore a bridle.

Carl Jans attached a rope, following Jessica's order of "no sudden movements" as he navigated around the black beast.

"Good, okay Lewis come to this side by me." Jessica positioned herself so she could get at the cow to help in the delivery while still trying to avoid being kicked.

Lewis Jans, the second of Carl Jans' sons, moved around to stand behind her.

"We have to do this fast, Carl."

No exchange was necessary. They understood the risks.

Jessica rolled up her sleeves and donned the glove for the procedure. "My guess is the calf is turned.

This was not a first. The Jans men had witnessed difficult deliveries. However, a woman in control had them more than a little worried.

Carl and Clark steadied while Lewis, at the other end with Jessica, watched her reach into the massive Angus.

The animal lifted her head and snorted.

The cow was not going to tolerate the discomfort for long.

"Okay we've got hoofs." Jessica adjusted her footing and began to move the calf.

Suddenly the Angus kicked, narrowly missing Jessica and a full blow to her torso.

"Okay, I'm pulling the calf or we'll lose both." Jessica didn't wait for a response as she inserted her gloved hand into the beast.

At first nothing, then two hoofs, slick and wet. Jessica's grip remained firm.

The Angus writhed, desperate to break free.

"Lewis!"

Lewis grasped the pair of calf's hoofs that protruded.

"Slow, Lewis. She's going to fight it." Jessica's hand disappeared inside the large animal. "Come on, stubborn little one."

Slithering from its mother, the calf landed softly in the hay at Jessica and Lewis' feet.

The Angus lay motionless and Jessica feared the worst.

The hoof flew glancing her rib cage, the blow sending

her stumbling backwards. The Jans' first instinct was to rush to help her.

"Don't let go of her!" Jessica, sprawled against the fence, got up.

Shock registered on all three.

Jessica blamed the sharp stabbing in her side on getting the wind knocked out of her. "She's carrying twins."

Jessica motioned for Lewis who had lifted the first calf out of harm's way. It was not unusual for a cow in the midst of a difficult delivery to stand up and accidentally step on or kick her newborn. Jessica was thankful for the care he had taken in insuring the first calf's survival.

She yanked off her soiled glove and slipped on a new one.

"Okay, if we're lucky this one's not breech. Are we ready?" Jessica glanced at the trio.

"Good girl," Jessica concentrated, speaking steady, in rhythm with her movements, as she examined the position of the second calf.

The Angus' overall appearance showed little improvement but she was not struggling as much.

"Okay girl, this one wants to meet the world the right way." Jessica's gloved arm guided the second calf onto the barn floor.

Lewis acted quickly, placing the newborn calf in the hay next to its sibling.

Carl and Clark Jans held fast.

Jessica knelt by the tired beast. "Carl, she may not pull through." Losing the mother was not unheard of. It didn't make it any easier. "I'm going to stay with her for awhile."

Jessica noted the apprehension in the new vet's ability had been replaced with appreciation.

A pang of sadness entered in. If only...

"Bottles for 'em?"

Lewis Jans' observation was based on years of experience. The Angus twins would be bottle fed in the event the mother didn't survive.

"Go ahead." Jessica dug in her bag. "But we'll hold off feeding for a little while." She didn't need to look at any of them. All shared in the hope of the cow's survival.

"I'll sterilize a couple bottles and get the formula handy," Lewis called over his shoulder as he headed out the barn door.

The extent of the kick's damage resonated through her entire body. *Move slow, McCabe.*

"Jess, you okay?" Carl Jans, half way down the hayloft ladder, dropped the bale to one side and jumped to the floor finishing his decent.

His proximity demanded she relax her clenched jaw to sell him on her condition.

"Your ribs are hurt, aren't they?"

Despite her effort, he saw the wince.

"No, just a little stiff." Jessica opened her bag. Pasting on a smile, she turned, stethoscope in hand.

"I bet you're hungry. Have you had any lunch?"

Jessica shook her head.

"Why don't we go up to the house and--"

"I'm fine, thanks anyway." Jessica, examining the cow,

observed Carl Jans' gesture to his son.

The senior Jans left the barn. He was getting her lunch whether she wanted it or not.

"Jonas would be proud of you, Jess."

The burning lump in Jessica's throat threatened to overtake her. "Thank you, Clark."

Jessica watched with cautious optimism as the hemorrhaging stopped and the Angus rested.

She knew the animal's condition was touch and go for the time being and as such decided to settle in for a while, perhaps even overnight.

The Jans family brought food to the barn despite her protests. The first bite of Thelma's homemade apple pie had just exploded on her taste buds as Andrew came through the door.

"You broke your damn ribs didn't you?"

Doctor Andrew Harrison's voice, cautious, startled Jessica, the attempt to disguise her injury exposed by a grimace as she jumped.

Leaning against the outside of the cow's stall, Jessica did everything in her power to maintain the illusion, nothing was wrong.

"Obviously Carl did more then bring me something to eat when he went to the house."

The old doctor set his bag on the floor.

Jessica put the piece of pie on the bale of hay next to her and lifted her shirt.

The bruise showed the promise of a kaleidoscope of

colors.

Jessica bit the inside of her cheek as Andrew examined her rib cage.

"You think I look bad, you should see the Angus." Jessica's shot at humor did not set well.

"Get in the car. You're going for x-rays right now." Andrew shoved the stethoscope in his bag.

"No I'm not." Jessica pulled her shirt down. "If they are broken, which they're not, all you can do is tape 'em up."

"Listen here young lady--"

"And you can tape 'em up here."

"I didn't think it was possible. You're more stubborn than your grandfather." Andrew huffed, exasperated. "I'll wrap you up. But you're coming in for x-rays." He marched out the barn door, no discussion.

Jessica picked up her plate of apple pie. A shockwave shot up her right side. "Okay," she gritted her teeth, "maybe they are broken."

The Angus progressed better than she expected. By early evening, Jessica felt comfortable leaving the Jans farm. She left strict instructions to call her if anything changed. Then promising to check on the Angus in the morning, Jessica steered her Jeep north to Doc Harrison's.

Andrew rewrapped the bandages and gave her some medicine for the night. She left for home with orders to meet him at the clinic in the morning for x-rays.

Although she hated succumbing to it, the painkiller made lying in bed tolerable. The drowsiness that accompanied its effects also made it easier to avoid the papers still covering the kitchen table from earlier in the day.

CHAPTER 15

The thumping sound she heard as her eyes met the first light of dawn was not her alarm. She leaned up on her elbow to check the clock, only to be christened with a sloppy lick.

"Thanks, Harv." Jessica wiped the slobber.

She got her bearings. It had been a late night, with her last veterinarian call ending at midnight.

Despite the rough initiation into taking over her grandfather's practice, Jessica had become immersed in the routine of being Gracier's local vet.

Day after day, she traveled the countryside dealing with the simplest to the more dramatic in vet calls, allowing the hectic schedule to be her refuge.

Coming down the stairs, Jessica realized she had not left the porch door open for Harvey.

"Sorry, boy." She looked around confirming he hadn't left any gifts for her on the kitchen floor.

Relieved, she flipped the coffee canister lid. "Okay, well." Jessica sighing, hung her head in mock defeat. "No coffee." She hadn't gotten groceries yet.

Up the stairs, she donned jeans, a sweatshirt and her favorite baseball cap.

"Harvey, you up for a trip to town?" Jessica swore she could see a smile on the dog's furry mug whenever a trip to town was announced.

They pulled up to the bakery as Samantha Caldwell flipped the sign on the front door to read "OPEN".

The chiming bells weren't unique to Samantha, the first customer on this Friday however was.

"Hey Sam." Jessica waved hello as she passed the threshold into the cozy confines of Caldwell's Bakery Shop, the smells intoxicating.

"Hey Jess." Sam returned the wave.

"Could I get a cup this morning?" Jessica slid into a booth at the front of the bakery by the large window that framed the town square, a choice spot for Sam's dedicated patrons.

Samantha grabbed a full pot from the coffeemaker on the front counter.

Its fresh brewed aroma Jessica craved.

"Join me?"

Jessica's invitation was welcome.

"You're in town early today."

Although a slight age difference, growing up in a small town assured little if any anonymity. And as would naturally happen, they had run into each other periodically over the last month.

No doubt, they had a lot in common, single women,

running their own businesses in a small town. Becoming friends seemed natural. She wondered if Sam Caldwell sensed the similarities.

"No coffee at home." Jessica shrugged her shoulders as Sam poured each a cup. The steam rolled off the dark liquid. "Thanks." Drawn outside the window, Jessica observed the small Midwest community coming to life.

Jonas had kept her "in the loop" with Gracier, Iowa happenings. He had sent flowers in their name when Sam's parents had died.

"That little Sam Caldwell, you remember her Jess, she's quitting her job in Chicago and moving back to run the bakery."

She wondered if Sam's reaction to small town life had been as Jessica's, a renewed appreciation for the beautiful simplicity of early mornings in Gracier, having experienced the other end of the spectrum in the city's hustle and bustle.

"How are the ribs?" Sam sipped from the steaming cup.

"They're getting better, a little twinge once in awhile." Jessica was not surprised by Sam's knowledge of her injury. The Jans were quick to spread the news on how she had saved the prize Black Angus and successfully delivered twin calves. She'd heard the story on almost every call since then.

"Lewis and Clark think you are it!" Sam winked at Jessica. They both chuckled.

The names the Jans' boys had been christened with, a manifestation of their father's fascination with early

American history, had resulted in more than a few remarks at the boys' expense growing up. And it would still get a laugh out of someone new to Gracier, but to the locals the expeditionary names, nothing extraordinary.

"Are you glad to be back, Jess?"

Sam's inquiry was not unusual. But Jessica had let her work demands absorb the days, averting the many questions darting in and out of her subconscious. It was not her nature to avoid and that troubled her even more.

Several weeks had come and gone since she and Andrew had gone through the lock box contents. At nights, Jessica used exhaustion as an excuse to avoid the myriad of items, not ready to face what the many papers and pictures begged to tell. Curiously, Andrew had not pushed the issue either.

"Sometimes it's like I never left," Jessica was subdued. She ran her finger around the cup's rim. "Then there are times..."

The light had all but chased the darkness away.

Jessica topped off the cups and rose to start a new pot brewing, a familiar task she had performed during her teenage years, waiting tables at Hannah's.

The young bakery owner accepted the unconscious gesture.

Jessica slid into the booth. "Does it ever become home again?" She studied Sam's sincere demeanor.

Sam ran a hand over the table, clearing away imaginary crumbs or pushing away what hit too close to home.

Jessica kicked herself. Maybe Sam wasn't experiencing the ease in their company as she was.

"There are moments...I still wonder..." Sam paused. "Yet every day I come to realize, this is where I'm supposed to be."

There was more. Something Sam wasn't sure she should say.

"At first it was tough."

Jessica perceived a gradual change. Sam relaxed. Without the required history, they were old friends who had found each other after years apart.

"I was heartbroken at the loss of my parents, angry at my brother and sister for not helping...and the prospect of having to close the shop all on my own..."

Sam disappeared into the back room. She returned, holding a handful of yellowed, tattered notes.

A grocery list, signed with a heart and the initials of Sam's mother, a faintly legible *"To The Love of My Life"* on a card that years ago must have accompanied a bouquet of flowers, a recipe scribbled in a faded blue ink that showed the wear and tear of floured fingerprints double checking measurements. Over a dozen notes told her parent's story. Two people who had spent a wonderful lifetime living, working, and loving each other all along the way.

Sam, having grabbed a pot, warmed the cups with fresh brew.

Jessica collected the pieces of paper to insure no coffee would mar their existence.

"I was here doing inventory, figuring out what to do with supplies and equipment. The realtor had contracted to list it. I opened a drawer, began to empty it and the recipe box..."

Jessica couldn't begin to imagine. Would she ever be able to look at the untouched, laid across her kitchen table with the same peace?

"My parents worked side by side for years. But how much that meant to me, how much I wanted what they had..."

Jessica watched Sam as she flipped through the small pieces of paper.

"They kept the recipe to a happy life with their recipe for cinnamon rolls." Sam smiled at Jessica. "Sorta puts it all into perspective."

The bakery bells chimed.

"Morning Miss Samantha, I--" Surprise and happiness broke the lines of Hannah Johnston's creased brow, showing delight at the early morning oddity.

"Well what better sight to greet these old eyes than my two favorite young women chatting, enjoying a cup of early morning coffee."

Not missing a beat, she claimed a cup and a seat. Jessica poured her a steaming cup.

"Wondered how long it would take, why, you're kindred spirits, cut from the same cloth, just like..." She stuck her thumb into her chest. "Me!"

Hannah accessed the papers. She hid nothing. She had seen them before. The tragic accident had stolen two of her dearest friends.

"The women of Gracier," Hannah's proclamation brought a smile to all three. "What's the latest with you two?"

"Well, we're pondering the insanity of two women

running businesses in this one horse town." Sam cocked her head. "And lo and behold--."

"It must be a sign." Hannah winked. "The three musketeers minus the mustaches and beards!"

Jessica laughed as the three raised their cups in salute.

They spent the next hour talking about nothing of great consequence, enjoying each other's company. Jessica, a member of this new trio, valued the bond that had begun to form.

As the bakery filled with early morning patrons, Jessica was impressed by the ease with which Sam traveled around the small shop, keeping her customers happy and fed.

She should move on with her day.

Jessica and Hannah bid their farewells. She was glad they had all agreed that this would be a standing Friday morning appointment.

Sam waved at the two women as they left the bakery. She could easily see why Steven Conrad was in love with her, she was stunning even at this early hour and easy to like. The woman she wanted to hate for always having his heart was becoming a friend.

***

Hannah accompanied Jessica to her Jeep. She was going to have to hustle to be ready by noon. The interruption had been well worth it. "How are things with our local vet?"

"Okay."

Hannah noticed Harvey curled up in the passenger's seat, basking in the early morning sun. He lifted his head at the sound of voices then placed it between his paws.

"Has Andrew said anything to you?" Jessica shielded her eyes from the day's early rays.

Friend to both Andrew Harrison and Jonas McCabe, many a slice of pie had been shared discussing life in general, sometimes specific, terms.

When Andrew showed up that day, well after the lunch hour, Hannah concluded something was up.

The reading of Jonas' will had occurred that day, her prayers relentless the entire morning. It hadn't revealed much more than the two had suspected.

Both had known Jonas' obsession. They had agreed barring Jessica discovering the information they hoped he had destroyed, it would remain buried in the old man's soul.

"He misses your grandfather a lot." Hannah looked over the square to her restaurant. "He's somewhat lost sitting in that booth."

Hannah tapped the Jeep door. "They'll all be lost if I don't get there pretty damn soon." She measured the tall young woman. "Why don't you join Doc for lunch today?"

The uncertainty in Jessica was visible.

"Okay, as long as it's fried and filling."

Jonas McCabe had given the identical order every noon hour for the last fifty years. His granddaughter's heartfelt impersonation brought a bit of healing.

Hannah headed across the street giving one last directive. "Get Sam on your way today. She never eats a decent meal. Maybe I can fatten you two other musketeers up."

Patting her round rear end, she hurried off in the direction of the cafe.

***

Much remained the same inside the cinder block walls of Cooper's Grocery. And that was quite alright.

The dinging bell prompted Raymond Cooper to look up from where he was stocking canned goods. "Well Doc, thought maybe you forgot how to get here." He marched up the aisle to Jessica and wrapped his big German arms around her. "Beginning to wonder if you were eating at all."

The gasp escaped her mouth before she could stop.

"Oh Hon, I'm sorry." Raymond quickly released his grip. "I forgot your ribs."

"Is there *anyone* in this town who doesn't know about my ribs?" She kissed his square, stout face. "They're not that bad."

A grin broke through.

Her grandfather had traded at Cooper's, one of her favorite trips to town as a child.

Adrienne Cooper, Mr. Cooper's wife, had always tucked a treat inside their grocery sacks. A hunt for the treasure, an adventure, every time Jessica and Jonas returned home.

"The Jans boys have been crowing for weeks now." The mischievousness was not to be missed. "If they weren't already married they'd be fighting over who got you."

"If only our sons had as much sense." Adrienne Cooper came from the back of the store. Taking Jessica's hand, she squeezed it in her warm grasp.

Jessica, imagining her own grandmother, often pictured

Adrienne Cooper.

"Well, I woke up and had no coffee this morning I knew I'd hit the bottom of the barrel." Jessica winked, ensuring the comment would divert the matchmaking conversation.

Raymond wagged his finger at her. "Well that tells me the chances of food left in that household are slim to none."

Adrienne put Jessica at arm's length and assessed her, top to bottom. "You are skin and bones!"

Raymond rolled a cart in front of Jessica. "You do not come to this register until your cart is full." The law had been laid.

Jessica wheeled the cart up the first aisle, "Where's the pop and potato chips?"

Adrienne despised "junk food". Her response was true to form. "That section is off limits, now keep yourself moving!"

Jessica felt normal if for only a moment.

She began to stroll the aisles, a "no-brainer" and somewhat relaxing.

She contemplated the frozen food aisle and the possibility of sneaking a pizza past the Coopers'.

"You received strict instructions not to purchase that junk."

Matthew was carrying a basket filled with fruit and vegetables.

"Working hard to score some brownie points?" She alluded to his basket overflowing with healthy contents. He was not in his usual "lawyer attire", as she'd seen him on the street or through a store window the last few weeks. Khaki's with a button-down his signature everyday wear.

"How are the ribs?"

Jessica opened the door to the freezer, uncomfortable at his reference to the injury.

"They're fine." She dropped a pizza into her cart. "Well, I'll be sure to checkout ahead of you so I don't have to hear how I'm not eating as well as the good Judge."

She watched somewhat amused as Matthew blushed at the use of his nickname.

"Don't forget to get your carrot juice in aisle three." She pushed her cart up the aisle and around the end.

"Okay young lady, what've you selected today?"

John Cooper, the eldest of the Cooper brood came from behind the meat counter to ring up her cart.

"And no, I won't divulge the junk food treasure trove you've acquired." The grocer's scolding frown broke into classic Cooper. "You're on your own if she spies it before you're out the door."

Jessica had run into John Cooper the first week back in Gracier, as he was always out in the community delivering groceries. He also held the special distinction, President of the local Chamber of Commerce.

"Big party tonight, Jess."

Today was the beginning of the annual Fall Fest in Gracier, which kicked off with a dance. Jessica had witnessed decorations promoting the event on display throughout the community.

"I bet a lot of folks would love to see you." John retrieved another brown paper sack. "What else do you have to do on a Friday night in grand old Gracier, Iowa?

Matthew walked up behind. Tension fired the space between. The memory of the last community dance attended was still raw.

"It's been a while since I've been on a dance floor, John."

He gave Jessica her change.

"Oh come on, Jess." John, groceries in each arm, came around the check out.

Jessica nodded a farewell to Matthew.

"I seem to recall someone who could 'shake her groove thing'."

He winked at her as she passed the door propped ajar by his foot.

"I'll be back in a second, Matthew!"

Matthew rubbed the stubble of his unshaven face. He couldn't help noticing how tired she looked.

It was all over town how the "the Doc's granddaughter" had stepped into the role of local vet without a hitch. He did not doubt her nonstop pace was serving its purpose.

Matthew had not seen much of her until today. He had made no effort to increase the likelihood of their meeting.

From the little he gathered in his brief conversation with Doc Harrison and the encounter with Jessica in the loft, the suspicion Jonas died with had yet to be discovered.

Matthew knew in his gut, Jonas was wrong.

***

"John Cooper!" Jessica hit the local merchant upside the head as he finished placing her groceries in the Jeep.

"All in a day's work, Doc." Saluting, he started then stopped, the confident smirk replaced with a sheepish grin. "Oh shit. Jess I wasn't even thinking about Matthew..."

Jessica teased a glimmer of forgiveness. "Don't worry. I have enough on you, John Cooper, to make your life a living hell until you're as old as Adrienne and Raymond."

She put the Jeep in gear and headed down the road.

***

Jessica was pulling into the lane when she saw Steven's red sports car. The dust cloud that kicked up behind it spoke to the land's need of rain.

The car was beside her as she hoisted the first sacks.

"It must be official, you're staying." Steven grabbed two bags.

She'd been avoiding the commitment. Purchasing supplies was a subtle indication. "Well at least until I run out of food."

Glancing back, she watched as Harvey jumped from his perch on the Jeep's passenger seat, out to explore the fields where many animals, their summer homes now harvested, ran the barren rows of black Iowa soil.

Placing the groceries on the kitchen table, Jessica caught Steven appraising the papers piled to one end.

Jessica hadn't mentioned the lock box or its contents since the day they sat in the loft surrounded by her mother's paintings. And Steven struggled with her uncharacteristic behavior. It was not like her to hide from what she needed to confront.

"So, are you headed to the big dance this evening?"

Jessica filling the pantry shelves, turned.

"Funny you should bring that up." Steven handed her more cans.

She continued to restock the barren cupboard.

"I'll pick you up early. We can get a bite to eat before we hit the dance floor."

"You, Mr. Conrad, have lost your mind." Jessica didn't miss a beat as she placed items in the refrigerator. "I don't do dances."

"Sorry, not accepting 'No' for an answer today. So you can come as you are or you can be dressed and ready."

Jessica wasn't in the mood to argue. Steven could come to pick her up, she'd feign a headache and he could go on without her.

"Yes Sir!"

"And don't try the 'I'm not up to it' monologue on me. All work and no play makes Jessica a dull girl."

She ignored him hoping he would drop it.

The "tone" he used was dead serious. "If I have to throw you over my shoulder and haul you there as is." He gave her a playful once over.

"Oh come on, Steven." Jessica was willing to resort to good old-fashioned begging. "I hate those things and--"

"You don't hate those things. It's the 'who' you might run into you hate."

Jessica sidestepped his brazen comment. "It's like I'm on display whenever I go into town."

"Well you are on display."

His brutally honest remark threw Jessica off guard.

Steven appeared just as surprised. "And nothing like a dance to give those good town folk something to chew on."

He stopped at the clock. "Whoa! Got an appointment I can't miss." Steven shrugged on his jacket. "I'll be here at 8:00 sharp."

She opened her mouth to protest. The door slamming stopped her short.

Jessica glared at the final grocery sack. She hated when he got the best of her.

Reaching in, she grabbed for the last item.

A bright yellow package of Juicy Fruit Gum...her favorite childhood treat.

Adrienne Cooper had remembered.

CHAPTER 16

As promised, Steven was at the door, 8:00pm sharp.

Jessica had gotten ready despite her petition to stay home. It did, however, feel good to get dressed up for a night out. She was not about to admit that to Steven.

"Okay, I'm up to get you in five, four, three, two, one--"

She descended, pirouetting. Her dress fluttered around her ankles. It was a simple dress, a nice change from her usual attire, plus she liked the way it fit.

Unlike most days out on call, she had decided to let her hair down.

"Wow!"

His approval had always meant a lot to her. She couldn't imagine a better "big brother".

"Won't you be a little chilly?" He pointed out her sleeveless shoulders.

"Yes brother, I have a shawl to wear." She rolled her eyes in mock exasperation.

A few short minutes and they were in front of Mickey's

for dinner. Jessica silently prayed they could drag the meal out and forget the whole event.

But much too quickly, she was thanking Mickey for another delicious meal, promising a dance for later that evening.

Cars filled the grounds around the fair barn and overflowed onto the street. John Cooper's hard work planning the annual event had more than paid off.

"Coop is pretty proud tonight." Steven chuckled. "I think I already hear crowing."

Steven opened the door for Jessica. His grin acknowledged her insistence in leaving the top down had resulted in quite the hairdo. Nevertheless, the wind that had tossed her hair into a maze of curls had felt wonderful.

"Is it too wild?"

"Let's go give the old boy some grief. We don't want him getting too full of himself."

In the barn and up the wide staircase leading to the dance on the second floor, the memories rushed at Jessica.

The smell of hay and hot apple cider, probably spiked by now, filled her nostrils. As difficult as it was, there was a sense of belonging.

The room was decorated with all the signs of fall. Pumpkins and gourds stacked on hay bales circled the perimeter. To the far end, the band was set up playing, music filling the air much to the dancers' delight.

Along the wall across from where they had entered was a table laden with homemade goodies to munch on. As her nose predicted, a container of hot apple cider simmered in the center of the trays heaped with food.

Tables and chairs set along the outside perimeter, left space in the center to dance.

"You mean you could actually find someone to come with you tonight?" John Cooper gripped Steven's outstretched hand.

"Running for mayor are we, Coop?" Steven slapped his friend on the back. "Quite a shindig you've put together to impress the local folk."

John Cooper faked a punch to Steven's midsection.

"Well Doc McCabe, you grace us with your presence." John Cooper offered his arm. "This calls for an honorary dance with the party chairman." He leaned in, "Can you 'shake that booty'?"

Jessica responded by swatting him upside the head. "Don't you get tired of picking on me, John Cooper?"

"Hey, I've got a few years to make up here, McCabe."

Her childhood nickname brought a smile.

"So work with me."

He spun her onto the dance floor.

She waved at Steven, as the barn floor's wooden planks whirled under her. The girl had emerged, carefree, assured, tension and frustration leaving her for the moment.

As he set his sights on a cup of hopefully spiked cider, Steven noticed Patty Ann buzzing about, replacing empty trays and testing the punch bowl contents.

Lord have mercy on the one who tries to spike the cider tonight.

Steven smirked as he envisioned the wrath that would be unleashed if any hooch got into her apple cider.

"Hey Patty Ann!" Steven twirled his mother around.

Greeted with a halfhearted frown, she scolded him with her free hand.

"You look like a lady who needs to dance with her son." Steven procured the platter of pumpkin bars from his mother and before she could protest, had her on the floor as the band broke into a polka.

Arthur Conrad smiled at his wife and son.

Simple things brought the most pleasure to the hometown folk. Regardless the age, everyone in attendance flocked to the dance floor when a polka tune filled the air. It didn't matter how hokey it was, or how cool some young people thought they were, cutting loose transcended inhibitions.

Those who could no longer gallop across the ancient wood floor tapped toes and canes in rhythm while workers manning stations at the food or beer table clapped along.

He yearned for that kind of contentment.

Applause erupted as the final accordion strain resounded into the rafters. Whoops and piercing whistles filled the room. Thoroughly winded, the polka participants cleared the floor ready for libation and a chair.

As the swarm parted, Steven saw Sam carting a platter of bakery buns to the kitchen where the ladies were assembling enough ham sandwiches to feed an infantry.

He did not miss how the dress sculpted her small frame.

Jessica leaned into Steven's ear. "She's kinda cute."

He could feel the creeping crimson.

"Yeah that Patty Ann is a looker."

Steven waved at his mother. Joy spread ear to ear from the turn around the dance floor with her son, Patty Ann Conrad was back at her assigned station.

Steven took note as a young man tucked a fifth of clear liquid into his shirt. The prankster disappeared into the crowd away from the apple cider.

"Nice try, Romeo." Jessica nudged Steven in the ribs. "Why don't you ask her to dance?"

Steven slid a chair out for Jessica.

"If you don't ask her to dance one of those Cooper boys will, and well my friend, as you know, one can't help but be enchanted by the Cooper charm."

Steven was not amused by the emergence of Jessica's mischievous streak. Adding fuel to the fire, John Cooper and his very pregnant wife arriving at the table catching the "Cooper charm" comment.

"Yes those Cooper boys know how to charm a lady." Kristine, John's wife, chimed in, patting her swollen belly for emphasis.

Steven, on his feet, pulled out a chair. "My dear Kristine," he hugged her, "the man has you totally fooled."

She returned Steven's welcoming hug.

"The Lord was watching over him."

"Yes, I am heaven sent." John Cooper playing it up puffed out his chest.

"Okay, it's getting deep in here." Steven, avoiding the original comment, stood up. "Who would like some 'spiked' apple cider?"

"Are you kidding me?" John Cooper shot up. "I told those kids--"

"Just yanking your chain, chief. Cider anyone? I'm buying."

Nods around the table signaled a tray would be required.

"Hon, you can't have any. Trust me." Steven winked at John's pregnant wife.

She smiled, understanding.

The space around the refreshment table was elbow to elbow. Constant chatter, wild gossiping, it was the hum of a beehive.

He wondered how much pertained to Jessica and hoped if it did, she wouldn't overhear any.

Even after years of tired rumors, knowing she had become quite hardened to it, it still bothered Steven.

The mob dwindled, and Steven was able to get three glasses filled with the "tasty drink".

"Could you pour me a cider?" He pointed. "That pitcher on the counter behind you please."

Steven's mother reached for the glass. The epiphany registered.

She set the empty glass down and helped herself to one of the three glasses he had just served up from the potent punch bowl.

"Now Patty Ann--" It was too late, the amber liquid had crossed her lips.

Steven, unconsciously wincing, primed for the other shoe to drop, was speechless as his prim, proper mother emptied the glass.

"I wish those boys would learn to use rum instead of vodka." She tossed the empty cup into the trashcan. "Be sure to give Kristine the right one." She ducked into the kitchen.

Steven stood astounded. This was not his mother.

"This should work." Sam Caldwell slid a tray in front of Steven. "And your mother said your limit is three."

The band started up, drowning him out as he tried to thank her for the tray. It didn't matter, as she was quick to turn back to the kitchen.

Her exit detoured however, as Harry Anderson, Gracier's local barber, offered an arm.

Well into his seventies, he still could do a mean fox trot, demonstrated in the way he skillfully guided Sam Caldwell onto the dance floor.

One after another of her male patrons waltzed with the young bakery owner. She lit up the room as well as the old souls she danced with.

"Even a happily married man like me looks twice." Steven's father stepped up beside his son.

Steven knew he couldn't play dumb with the senior Conrad.

"You might check on Patty Ann, she's been in the cider." Steven nudged his father en route to his table.

He arrived to find John and Jessica out on the dance floor, having left Kristine to watch.

"So he's left you for another woman." Steven set the alcohol free drink in front of her. "I'd be more than honored to dance with you."

Though visits home rare, he had gotten to know her quite well. He loved hanging around their house. Steven hassled John relentlessly about his ever-increasing herd. A part of him, though, would be quite happy with the small-town life this man and wife shared.

"I'm not exactly 'light on my feet'."

A ballad began.

"No excuse." Placing his hand under her elbow, they walked, in Kristine Cooper's case, waddled to the dance floor.

They had just taken a few steps when the tap occurred on his shoulder.

"Now, I know you're lonely pal, but by wife? Miss Caldwell, do you mind?"

Steven turned to the pair.

"He's kind of awkward, have pity." John Cooper with one smooth motion whisked his wife away.

"Don't worry, you're off the hook, the ladies are pretty busy back there."

"You're not in charge of the wine bottles, are you?" Steven cut short Samantha Caldwell's exit from the awkward situation.

They began to dance, falling into the rhythm of the band.

"Did you get a tetanus shot?" Steven's arm encircled her waist. The sensation he fought that night at her home possessed him.

"Ah yes, what every girl wants whispered into her ear."

Without a comeback, Steven fixed on the people dancing around them and in doing so caught John Cooper's triumphant stare.

Always playing matchmaker. Would it never end? Steven shot a look that should have stopped his old friend cold, but John Cooper was too busy gliding Kristine around the floor, enjoying the coup.

***

Jessica weaved her way off the dance floor after a rousing polka with John Cooper followed by the twist with Chester.

Patty Ann motioned her over to the punch bowl.

Thanking her for the beverage, she headed to the window, the evening breeze blowing softly through her hair and the folds of her dress a welcome indulgence.

"You haven't lost your ability to, what did John call it, 'shake your booty'?"

Jessica nearly dropped her cup. Matthew's intense gaze did not release her.

She embraced the shadows that draped. This was exactly why she battled coming tonight.

"Well, John has a few moves left in him I'll admit."

John shot her a raised eyebrow. She could only imagine what they must be thinking.

No, I am not doing this. I've come too far. His arrogant presence was not going to throw her anymore. Andrew's advice carried her.

"Well, it'd be a shame to waste good music." Jessica set her drink on the windowsill.

The tempo slowed.

Damn! Jessica silently cussed the musicians. She was

trying to maintain the upper hand. *Could they cooperate?*

"Do you do this sort of thing anymore?" Jessica, with one hand on Matthew Cassidy's shoulder, slipped the other into his palm. "You're getting on in years." Familiar defiance, it felt good.

"I manage."

"Heads up." Escorting his wife, John Cooper scanned the crowd for Steven.

"Oh-oh." He looked at his wife searching, and tilted his head.

Sam and Steven, still on the floor, were on a collision course with Matthew and Jessica.

Shrugging his shoulders, John put his arm around Kristine and strolled to the table. "Let the games begin."

***

"Mr. Cassidy, I believe you promised me a dance this evening."

Matthew nodded at Sam's invitation before guiding her away.

"Why do you do that to yourself?" Steven did not attempt to hide his contempt and anger.

He placed his arm around Jessica's waist. "Man, Jessica I--"

"Don't," Jessica, although quiet, was firm. "I will not hide in a corner afraid of running into him. I'm not that naive little college girl anymore, Steven."

There was nothing he could say to her renewed confidence.

The music segued to one of their favorite tunes. With the drummer pounding out the beat, he spun her, breaking into a "skin the cat" routine that upon the song's conclusion left both breathless.

"Little too much for you, Conrad?"

Steven flopped into a chair ignoring her dig.

"The ladies room calls. Refills anyone?" Jessica glanced at each of them. "Okay, I'll be back, after I find myself an unoccupied kybo."

Steven shooed her off half-heartedly as she flaunted how unfazed she was by their wild spin around the dance floor.

"You handled yourself well."

Steven, in no mood for John Cooper's comments, drained his drink and left the table for a refill.

***

The night air outside the barn caressed Jessica.

The line was longer than her bladder cared to wait. In true Iowa farm girl ingenuity, she sized up the stand of trees and bushes at the far end of the barn. Moments later, she came from behind her improvised "powder room".

"Once a farm girl, always a farm girl."

Jessica tripped on the uneven ground.

Matthew knelt beside her. "Sorry, I didn't mean to scare you."

She could see his genuine concern in the moonlight.

He stood.

Jessica accepted his help and gathered her footing, brushing off her dress.

His fingers in her hair reappeared with a twig from the

bushes.

The emotions she had proudly mastered were unraveling.

"I'm okay, Matthew." She pleaded with the dark night to hide her face.

"I need to talk to you, Jessica."

She started walking.

"Did you hear me, Jess? We need to talk."

There was no halt in her gait.

"It's about the loft."

Jessica spun around. "Understand, Matthew," her manner was steady, "there is nothing I could possibly *need* from you. I have no idea why Jonas decided to trust you. Personal experience, you can't be."

Jessica wondered if he could sense her contempt.

Turning, she stepped and he was in front of her.

Jessica began to go around him, determined in her mission.

Matthew reached for her.

The sharp gasp sucked in the night air.

"Jess, your ribs, I forgot--"

"Let me by, Matthew." *Don't lose it.*

He stepped to one side.

She started towards the barn and Steven.

"I have never stopped loving you, Jess."

Jessica kept walking.

***

Steven had first seen the two figures as he looked out the barn window, wondering where she could be.

He bounded the stairs two at a time, rounding the corner to see Chester helping Jessica into his pickup.

Hank Anderson, waving them on, spotted Steven.

"She said to tell you she wasn't feeling well and she'd catch up with you tomorrow."

***

Reaching for the pickup door, he felt the hand on his shoulder. The grip was followed by a punch to his jaw, throwing him against the hood of the truck.

"Stay away from her," Steven's voice was low and menacing.

Matthew had long awaited this confrontation. Blood, salty, trickled into his mouth. "Keep out of this, Steven."

Ducking underneath the punch, he heaved Steven Conrad's towering frame into the air, slamming him into the pickup box.

Steven didn't move.

Matthew backed away. He couldn't be angry with him for protecting her.

"Somehow you fooled Jonas. But you won't fool her. You will not have her, Matthew." Shrugging off Matthew's hold, Steven planted both feet on the ground, his long stride carrying him away.

"I can't have her," Matthew looked out into the infinite blackness of the night sky, "she's my sister."

Steven halted, rigid. Matthew knew he was trying to take in the declaration that hung in the night air.

"You love her, Steven."

There was no break in the man's demeanor.

"I pray to God that will help you keep the truth from her." Matthew slid behind the wheel and fired the engine. Staring out over the hood, he put the pickup into gear.

The tall figure he left standing in the middle of the grassy field didn't move.

***

Matthew unlocked the door to his law office. Sitting down, he tugged the chain on the small green and brass lamp, its light filling the desk's oak expanse with a white glow.

Inserting the smallest key on the ring into the bottom left drawer, he opened it and pulled out a gray metal box. A second box, much smaller, covered in blue velvet, was tucked in the farthest corner of the desk drawer. His fingers touched the plush exterior, unopened since that day.

Shutting the drawer, he opened the lid to the gray box on his desk and the contents he'd been through countless times.

He prayed the papers would finally divulge what he desperately wanted, to prove Jonas McCabe's suspicions wrong.

The velvet box called, taunting the ember of hope to ignite.

CHAPTER 17

Jessica gave Chester the okay sign as she shut the back door. Pickup lights illuminated the lane as she grabbed a glass and a bottle of wine.

The road dust had settled. Chester was well on his way.

Angry with herself, the loss of control in his presence fueled Jessica's desire to put as much distance between her and the memories as she could. The wine she carried insured the goal.

Jessica unlocked the office door, laid the keys on the desk and filled the glass with wine. She took a drink of the dark burgundy liquid.

Her desk was filled with papers she had been avoiding, some hers, some Jonas'. Paperwork was the one part of running your own veterinarian practice that she hated. It had been weeks since she had sent bills, or for that matter, paid any.

"McCabe, you are a piece of work," Jessica broke the stillness. "In love with a man you can't trust." She tipped back in the chair speaking to the emptiness. "And by golly." She downed another drag from her glass. "He still loves you." Hot tears welled as the words escaped her once again, "Loves you."

Jessica opened the top right desk drawer where the ledger was kept. The discovery she'd made among the paintings that day accidentally slid out from hiding.

Her fingers extended, tentative. She hadn't read the letter after that day. Written for someone else, her intrusion, disquieting, had kept her away. The longing to learn more about Maggie trumped, until now.

The author's elegant signature, beautifully written at the bottom of the yellowed page, she had never seen up until the loft.

> *I write this frightened someone will see it and yet in hope it will find its way to you and into your heart. Always know, you are the reason I am here and for this life, we created.*
>
> *My devotion is unyielding. And though others may try to lessen its meaning, it is a lifetime worth of love.*
>
> *You must maintain loyalty to your dreams but in my soul, you will remain. And in this child, our love will live forever.*
>
> *Maggie*

"We are a pair, Mom." She tipped the wine bottle

refilling the half-empty glass. "Both in love with men we can't have--" her voice caught. "Or who don't want us." The page's content blurred.

The letter did not address anyone. Nevertheless, Jessica knew it was written to her father.

As she put the rim to her lips, the wine filled her senses but it could not stop the path her heart chose. Memories, a kaleidoscope she had worked to numb herself to, pricked at every scar laid bare.

Matthew's confession on that winter day had opened up a world to Jessica she had denied. Yet each had dealt with uncertainties, his their age difference, hers, family loyalty. One she foolishly considered was hers alone.

The small box was covered in deep, rich blue velvet. Jessica pretended not to notice it on the desk. He hadn't been expecting her.

Matthew tucked it away.

She prayed it would not make another appearance until the weekend was over.

Matthew had completed his internship, and Jessica had one class left of her summer course load. They were going home this weekend to face their families.

While they had decided to cross that bridge together, she was apprehensive.

Jessica watched as Matthew hurried around the apartment packing. He wouldn't admit it, but he was as nervous as she was.

"Jess," his deep voice traveled from the bedroom. "I'm

heading home as soon as I'm done here." He walked into the kitchen where she sat doing some last minute studying. "I hope that's okay?"

"I thought we had decided---"

"I know, I just...I would feel better if I could maybe..."

She moved to him. His arms, the perfect fit, her body to his, pushed the anxiety of the weekend to the farthest corners of her mind.

"Don't start without me okay?" She smiled up at him and winked.

Neither planned on the upcoming "event" going well. She also knew he liked to be well prepared. If there was ever a day to be ready for it was tomorrow.

Jessica helped Matthew load his bags in the truck.

He hushed within her curls. "You are hard to leave."

Her head on his chest reveled in the feel, his heartbeat.

Reaching for the door, he jumped in. "We okay?"

"Always." Through the rolled down truck window, she kissed him. "Now go."

He waved out the window as he rounded the corner and drove north.

Back in the kitchen, Jessica returned to her studies.

Arriving at the acreage later that day, Jessica could see Jonas sitting at the kitchen table. Contentment settled in her as she spotted Andrew and Chester's vehicles parked in the lane.

The evening was filled with laughter as the three special men reminisced. Not new to her, the tales of their antics still *sparked laughter.*

She jumped when the phone rang.

Jonas excused himself, leaving the supper table.

"Jessica, phone."

Getting up, she headed into the kitchen.

Jonas was strangely somber as he gave her the receiver.

"Hello?"

"We should talk before tomorrow, Jess."

"Nervous, huh?" She couldn't help teasing Matthew.

They had decided to tell each family about the relationship separately. Joseph and Jonas in the same room was a stretch. In the same room hearing their news was beyond imagination.

Jonas stood outside the doorway to the kitchen, aware something was up.

"I know we said in the morning, but I think it's best if I talk with Jonas tonight. I've--"

Matthew interrupted, void, flat, "It's up to you, Jess."

"I'll drive myself in after?"

"I better go."

He hung up without saying anything more.

A pang of anxiety reverberated.

Not long after, Andrew and Chester left, and she joined her grandfather on the front porch.

"You okay?"

He read her like a book.

"Yes and no."

"I'm guessing it has to do with the phone call." He drank his lemonade.

She hoped this was a night he had decided to add a little "kick" to his drink.

"I'm not going to pretend I don't recognize his voice, Jess. I've known that boy his whole life." Her grandfather stared straight ahead.

"We're in love." Her pulse thudded in her ears.

"Jessica, your happiness is the most important thing to me." He stopped. "It's not about this old man, honey." Standing up he walked to the porch railing.

Steeled for every argument, there was none.

He turned and hugged her.

Jessica now understood "floating on cloud nine".

Pulling into the fairground's parking lot, she spotted Matthew leaning against his pickup, holding a small object.

Her heart almost stopped. Although dark, the street light illuminated the area and the flash of blue velvet.

She shut the engine off before walking to him.

His hand went into his pocket and returned to the light, empty.

He looked at her in a way she couldn't describe. As if he had never seen her before. Then a stranger spoke.

"We've made a mistake, Jess." He looked right through her. There are things we...I can't get past and..."

Jessica was unable to hear the music that filled the air. The glow of the barn windows and the smell of the delicious food faded into blackness.

Driving out of the fairgrounds, she passed a man

holding a small blue box.

Treading just above the surface, a person near drowning, she stopped. "Enough." Setting the glass down resolute, she addressed the impending paperwork.

Reaching for the first stack of unfinished bills, Jessica's shawl snagged the wine glass, spilling it onto the piles of papers and over the side of the desk next to the wall.

Running through the door to the barn, she pulled some rags from the supply closet.

Jessica first dabbed the papers on the desk, separating them, then, knelt on the floor to wipe up the small puddles of wine.

The manila envelope, exactly like those in the lock box, hung wedged between the desk and the wall.

Wine dripped as she removed the envelope's contents.

***

What in the hell had Steven just heard? From Matthew's statement, Jessica had no idea...*or did she?*

The office light on, he parked the red sports car in front. Steven peered in the window, fully expecting to see Jessica, but met with a much different scene.

On the desk sat an empty wine bottle.

"Jess, you here?"

Nothing.

He called again, "Jess!"

Steven walked to the door that led into the rest of the building. It was dark.

Back at the office door, he looked once more to the

house, no light and no Jeep.

He turned toward the desk and saw the half-empty wine glass and the papers.

The photocopied articles, grainy, but the headlines stood out as boldly as the day they were printed.

Body of St. Mary's Student Found

Steven locked on the picture below the headline. Chester's face, considerably younger, the caption accompanying confirmed his identity.

> *"Sheriff Caughlin surveys the potential crime scene."*

Steven's eyes pored over the article.

> *The body of a St. Mary's student was found early Saturday morning in a ravine near Kelly's Ridge. Witnesses stated the victim had either fallen or been thrown into the deep ravine.*
>
> *A source close to the department stated evidence pointed to the possibility of foul play. Sheriff Caughlin had no comment.*

Finishing the article, Steven became riveted on the date, June 18, 1963, the day Jessica was born. He flipped the page.

Body Identified

(Gracier, IA-June 20, 1963) Local officials verify the body found in a ravine near Kelly Ridge is that of Peter Randall, a junior at St Mary's. Officials stated that an autopsy is being performed on the victim's body.

Randall was last seen on the campus Friday afternoon at approximately 3:00 pm. According to Randall's roommate, Randall left the dorm at approximately 7:00 pm that evening. He had seemed upset and stated he may not be back that night.

School officials were unaware of Randall's disappearance until contacted by the Lancaster County Sheriff's Department on Sunday morning, June 19.

The investigation reaffirmed fears that foul play may have played a part in Randall's death. As of press time, there are no leads in the case. However, evidence gathered indicates the death occurred at or near the scene. Sheriff Caughlin declined to comment on the case.

Randall has Local Ties

(Gracier, IA-June 27, 1963) The recent finding of a young man's body near

Gracier hits close to home. Peter Randall is the son of former residents Thomas and Clara Randall. The Randalls of Earlton, Iowa, formerly of Gracier, were notified of their son's death on the morning of Sunday, June 19.

Mr. Randall declined to comment on his son's death. Friends of the Randalls stated the family was shocked and overcome with grief.

A memorial service for the late Peter Randall is pending autopsy results.

Sheriff Still Silent

(Gracier, IA-July 5, 1963) The small community of Gracier remains in the dark on the mystery surrounding the death of young St. Mary's junior, Peter Randall, whose body was discovered the morning of June 18.

In a phone interview with Sheriff Caughlin, no new information was released. The Sheriff would not corroborate or deny any rumors circulating throughout the community.

Investigators from various state crime agencies were seen at the site throughout the last week. Officials are keeping a lid on whether anything was recovered.

Evidence Damaged Case Goes Unresolved

(Gracier, IA-July 25, 1963)Authorities announced today that due to mishandling, crucial pieces of evidence surrounding the mysterious death of St. Mary's student Peter Randall had been destroyed.

Sheriff Caughlin, in a press conference late Friday afternoon, stated information gathered was inconclusive and those who first came upon the body had inadvertently contaminated the scene. He also noted due to the heavy storm that moved through the area that night, potential evidence may have been washed away.

State officials at the press conference added they could neither confirm nor deny foul play in the young man's death, only that the case would remain open pending further investigation.

Present at the press conference were Thomas and Clara Randall, parents of the victim. In their only statement to the media, the Randalls asked that anyone with any information regarding their son's death to please come forward. The Randalls, shaken by the ordeal, were ushered out.

The press conference concluded with officials again asking for help.

Sheriff Caughlin, showing the effects of exhaustion after weeks of investigation, had no further comment.

The last news article fell from Steven's fingertips onto the desk. "Dear God, Jess..."

***

Wide-awake, unable to sleep, the sound of the small red sports car relayed up the tree lined street penetrating her dim cocoon.

His moonlit silhouette was unmoving. Then, suddenly, he opened the car door.

Though every logical bone in her body told her not too, she went to greet the late night visitor.

His hand ready to knock missed its mark.

"Hey Sam." His usual confidence was absent. "I know it's kinda late..."

Sam's greeting, a disconcerting silence, he crossed the Caldwell threshold, into the warm inviting atmosphere.

A blanket lay tossed covering the arm of the chair. His eyes went to the clock above the fireplace. "Sam, I'm sorry, I didn't mean to--" his apology missed, catching her exiting the room.

Sam reappeared with two beers, placing one on the end table closest to him.

He looked up from the overstuffed couch to deliver another "wine incident" comment. Samantha Caldwell's intoxicating beauty met Steven, unprepared.

Embers smoldered in the bottom of the fireplace. Taking some tinder, Sam positioned more wood using the fire iron, kindling the fire.

Steven approached. Her petite frame vibrated with tension.

He put his beer on the mantel.

"Okay, broken glass is one thing, setting your nightgown on fire is a whole nother story." He acquired the metal iron. Instinctively, his hand rested on her back.

Sam moved away.

He glanced at Sam standing, holding her beer, staring out into the night.

"Why are you here, Steven?"

"Who else would put up with me?" Steven shifted the burning log. "I guess you're filling in for Michael." He tossed a boyish grin her way.

"I'm not Michael."

She came at him, hand thrust forward.

Steven did not yield the fire iron.

The anger she radiated was unmistakable, the weeks of pretending over.

He tipped her chin up and looked into her beautiful, determined eyes.

"Don't do this to me Steven, I--"

The fire iron was leaned against the fireplace as he pulled her to him, kissing her. It was well hidden, nevertheless it was there, flowing, her body to his.

She pulled away. "I'm not a consolation prize, Steven," Her command, a footnote of resolve.

Her meaning clear yet his was hardly a secondhand response.

Steven had caught himself observing Sam in every situation that threw them together. Constantly on his mind, her face was the one he saw whenever he closed his eyes.

It had confused him at first, but as time passed, something he could not have imagined a few months ago was all he wanted, drawn to the strong willed figure.

"You have no idea what you're saying, Sam." His fingertips found her. The wetness of her cheek unveiled his heart. "Oh, Samantha Caldwell," he caressed her name. Its effect carried across her.

Sam crossed the room to the front door. His steps were quick behind her. He sensed her composure, reined in, if only by a thread.

His hands on her shoulders, pain was all he saw. *You are an ass, Conrad.*

Sam opened the door.

He stepped out to the porch. "Sam, I didn't mean to --"

Samantha Caldwell shut the door.

He fought the urge to push the door open and take her in his arms.

At the edge of the porch, he looked back. Her small frame knelt by the fire. He didn't need to see to know, the hands holding her face were wet with tears.

***

Jessica was unsure why she had driven here. The confusion engulfed her as it had that night.

Candles flickered, prompting shadows to dance in and

around the soft features of the Virgin Mary as she cradled her blessed son in her arms.

Walking up the center aisle to the statue, she knelt before the beautiful blue Madonna.

Even after years of turning her back on this, her faith, it welcomed her presence. She accepted the invitation, anguish leaving her to fall upon the altar.

The first rays of the brilliant Iowa dawn glimmered through the stained glass. Jessica's tortured night had lapsed into day.

He had seen Jessica as she slipped into the church, awakened by her Jeep in the predawn hour.

Finishing his morning rosary, the church's rear door creaked. Hinges in need of a good oiling served their purpose.

The priest prayed she had found what she came for.

CHAPTER 18

The sun forced his eyes to meet the day. Matthew raised his head from the desk, his bed for the night, papers spread out, a makeshift pillow.

Picking up, he put them safely away.

Coffee, black and strong, was required after last night.

The bakery lights called his name as he walked the sidewalk hugging the edge of Gracier's town square.

Sam's head was not feeling the best on this Saturday morning, for more reasons than the liquor.

The dinging bell was more than she could handle.

"Hey Sam."

Placing the hot pan of rolls on the center island to cool for icing, she headed to the front of the bakery.

"Morning, Matthew." She stopped short, taking in his disheveled appearance, positive he had not changed clothes since last night. "Whoa, Mr. Cassidy--"

"Yeah, I can about imagine." Matthew, behind the

counter, filled a cream-colored ceramic mug. "I'll buy you a cup." He nodded, recognizing her work.

"You got a deal."

They moved to the fragrant bakery kitchen.

She began to mix the rich white icing while Matthew topped off the mug set on the counter next to her.

"Danced until dawn, eh?" Over her shoulder, she appraised his attire.

"Yeah, you know me, out all night lookin' for fun."

The remark spoofing his clean-cut image did not match the disturbed, tired man.

Sam put down the frosting and wiped her hands on a towel. "Okay, what's up?"

He stared all too intensely into the dark black liquid that filled his cup. She knew without asking where his mind was.

"Jess was in yesterday. How is she doing?"

The true attorney, even when it was so very personal. Sam's instincts had served her well.

Sam deliberated, treading carefully. Observing them dance the night before, there was a line neither dared to cross.

She sipped from the steaming mug. "Matthew, I don't know what went on between you two."

The troubled man shifted.

"But I have never seen two people try harder not to be together."

Matthew ran his hand through his hair, stalling.

She'd seen it in Steven. It was the final straw.

"You and Steven are a pair." Cup on the counter she

returned to the bowl of frosting, whipping angrily at the white froth.

Sam stopped mid whip. "I don't get it. He loves her and can't tell her. You love her and won't have her." She resumed beating, furious.

"I believe this would be the 'pot calling the kettle black'." He folded his arms.

Her outburst had exposed too much.

"Does he even have a clue as to the amazing woman he's letting get away?"

"Nothing to know. Nothing to tell." She prayed he would let it drop.

"I love her more than I can..." his voice, sorrow. "But I made a promise."

The bell to the shop rang.

Walking out to wait on her latest customer, Sam heard the back door to the shop slam.

***

Steven Conrad had spent the rest of the night staring at his bedroom ceiling. The cracks in the plaster more tangled than ever, like his thoughts, trying to make sense of what he had read at Jonas McCabe's desk.

He wasn't sure what had led him to Sam's. *Or was he?*

The sting was still fresh. He had selfishly hurt the woman he had fallen in love with.

Sitting up on the edge of the bed, Steven addressed his reflection in the mirror. "You are an idiot."

He listened for the sounds of his parents' early morning ritual.

Nothing. They had already left for their Saturday morning stroll.

Dressing in jeans and a sweatshirt, Steven hurried to achieve a clean get-a-way before the "post dance inquisition".

He was the library's first patron today.

The original 1963 papers were yellowed, but the information they yielded had not faded.

Standing at the counter, Steven was struck by what the librarian had said.

"How odd, not many people request these old papers. They seem to be of interest lately, though."

Steven scanned the register to find the signature of the last to view the archived newspapers, Jonas McCabe.

Leaving the library parking lot, he had fully intended to head to the farm.

It was well into the day, after the last of her morning crowd that the bell rang.

"I'll be right there with your rolls." Sam maneuvered through the doorway to the front of the shop with Hannah's usual order. "I threw in a couple dozen extra since it was a little crisp this morning, I guessed you would get more chili eaters today and--" Sam stopped short.

Steven stood at the counter.

***

Aspirin for her headache and caffeine to keep alert. There was a lot of work to do this morning.

Sporting Levi's and a pullover, she filled the mug she

usually took on vet calls with dark, hot coffee.

Jessica popped two aspirin into her mouth, washed the tablets down and headed out to the office.

The doorknob held no resistance. She had left without locking it. Jessica gave the room a once over.

Her eyes came to the articles that lay on the desk. The wine spilled on the bills had cured to a faint purple stain.

The papers were not what she had come for. Jessica, up the loft stairs, unlocked the padlock to the room she had not been in since the day of the reading.

Switching on the light, she set her coffee safely to the side and started through the paintings.

***

Sam set the rolls on the counter.

Steven felt helpless. A trait he was not accustomed to. *Could she tell? Could she comprehend how this was killing him?*

No pity reflected. Only something he could not stand to see.

"I've got to explain to you. I'm--" Steven stopped as Sam went back to the kitchen.

"There's nothing to explain, Steven."

In the doorway, he watched, as she moved around the bakery kitchen, his presence nothing more than a brief interruption in another ordinary day.

It settled in his gut. A first in his admittedly arrogant, usually over-confident life...he was frightened.

Steven ran through his mind all he wanted to say to her. What he needed her to know.

He entered the kitchen, prepared to be ignored. Her unwavering stare greeted him instead.

"Something's going on with Jess." Slowly, deliberately, she wiped her hands on the dishtowel.

"Samantha, I am an idiot and I--."

"Matthew was in here today." She laid the towel down. "And my hunch is he's wrestling with the same thing you are."

She lifted herself up on to the counter. "I'm guessing from the little Jess has told me it has to do with Jonas. And somehow it all links back to Matthew."

Steven stood dumbfounded. Jessica should hear it first. But the idea of running his suspicions by Sam seemed somehow okay. He had a lot to work through, before he rocked Jessica's world.

Sam's face was a misinterpretation of his silence.

Open your mouth. Say it. I've fallen—-

"I won't argue the 'I am an idiot' part. The rest is up for discussion." Sam walked to the beeping oven.

***

Jessica flipped past each canvas, unsure where she had seen it.

Finally, in the third stack against the wall the light shed, illuminating.

She pulled it out, closer to the light. Kneeling, Jessica removed the article from her pocket. Her heart pounded and began to encompass her entire being. She couldn't breathe.

***

Sam finished reading the last article and laid it on the

counter. "What does this have to do with Matthew?"

She had asked the question that had driven him, but for reasons Sam was yet unaware.

Regardless of her reserve, the tension his proximity created could not be denied. The knot twisted tighter.

"I'm not sure..." Stubble, rough on Steven's hand served as testimony to his sleepless night. "I'm not sure of anything anymore."

Sam's jaw tightened. The wall was up.

He grasped her shoulders. "You don't understand, Sam."

Tears hovered, affirming what he had done. She tried to pull away.

His firm hold was turning her torment to anger.

The phone rang, breaking the standoff.

Steven grudgingly let go.

"Caldwell's Bakery," Sam revealed nothing to the caller. "Hi Patty Ann, yes he's right here."

His mother, always able to pinpoint the Conrad men's whereabouts, another of her uncanny gifts. He took the receiver Sam held out.

"Hey." Steven listened as his mother spoke. "When did she call? Ok."

He placed the phone on the hook.

Sam looked out the bakery's kitchen window. The sun was ascending to midday, casting a brilliant golden glow.

Steven was captivated.

"She needs you."

She let it spill over, descending, dripping from her jaw

as she dove into the lukewarm water to wash the last few morning dishes. The front bell rang, confirming his departure.

***

Seeing the door open, Steven headed straight for the office. The sounds above signaled where he would find her.

His heartbeat quickened as he ducked his head and stepped into the room filled with the paintings.

Sitting, encircled by the articles, Jessica did not move.

He followed her gaze. Initials disclosed the artist's identity hidden in the brush strokes at the bottom right corner.

"Is this my father, Steven?"

Steven could not take his eyes from the painting.

"And if it is, who killed him?"

Peter Randall's portrait was a work of passion, a young man in his prime, the youth of his early twenties captured perfectly. The desire felt in the painting of this picture, undeniable.

"Jess, I..." Steven struggled, unsure.

Patty Ann, only on rare occasions, mentioned her brother, his Uncle Peter. The growing realization, the reason behind her limited reminiscing was quickly turning into a sickening fear.

Steven battled his imagination as it tried to conceive the worst behind Jonas McCabe's possession of the articles and their key to a horrifying secret.

She sat eerily resolute. The trembling he had witnessed earlier had stopped.

"Read them, you..." She fixed on his hands and copies of the news articles he had gotten that morning from the Gracier Library archives. "I know who he is, Steven."

"Where did you find these?" Steven knelt beside her, and the articles.

"On the floor between Jonas' desk and the wall." Jessica paused. "I'm guessing they were knocked to the ground when he had his..."

He watched the anguish appear.

"This is what haunted him...what killed him, Steven." The pieces, the link, came full circle. "Peter Randall's death and my mother."

Matthew Cassidy thundered in Steven's head. Something held him back.

"Jess, Patty Ann...she..."

His head was spinning. *How could Patty Ann have kept this hidden...?* A chilling reality ran through Steven. *Does she know?* The potential it had to destroy so many lives fell over him, a smothering blanket.

"I think it's best for her to hear it from you first. She deserves it, Steven..." Jessica's voice trailed off.

She was right, but the bullheaded woman had a mind of her own. Could he trust her to stay put? Or would he come back to find her gone again? Even worse, where would she go and what might she find?

She sat transfixed on the items.

"You shouldn't be alone." He rose. "We'll go in the house and--"

"Steven." Jessica stood up and wrapped her arms around

him.

He held her without conflict.

"I'll get cleaned up. When you're ready, I'll head into town."

Steven held Jessica at arm's length. "Promise me you won't do anything until we talk with her?"

The half-hearted smile would have to do. His solace, she wouldn't hear what he had to ask.

In front of the painting, news articles spread on the floor, Jessica picked up one after another, desperate to memorize every detail. Hoping to be pointed away from the obvious.

Out the barn window, Jessica could see the thick cloud of dust hovering behind Steven's car.

Gathering the papers, she headed down the steps to her Jeep and drove out the lane.

CHAPTER 19

He turned at the sound of her Jeep. Grabbing a rag from the tool bench, he walked out of the shed.

Matthew's presence at the dance had tested her, but he was taken aback at her manner.

"Chester, I need to know about Peter Randall and my mother."

He methodically wiped the motor oil from his hands.

Jessica, out of her vehicle, thrust the articles at him.

The memory was as black as the ink in which they were printed. The stoic front, practiced for years regarding this subject, maintained.

"Let's go in the house."

The smell of coffee filled the air. He'd started a second pot for the day before going outside to putter in the yard.

He reached over the dishes, remnants of an early morning breakfast, and grabbed another cup for his guest.

Pushing the *Des Moines Register* morning edition to one side, he filled both cups. Sitting down he encountered the papers she had put on the table.

The papers, their pictures, weren't necessary. All was branded in his mind.

"They were on the floor next to Jonas' desk."

He knew the unflinching glare and the results it commanded, it was a tactic he'd practiced for years as county sheriff. Waiting for any hint, a crack in the veneer.

"I'm guessing they dropped there accidentally, the night he had the stroke." Jessica reached into her pocket. She placed the yellowed paper into his wrinkled hands. It was the letter, Maggie's letter.

Chester's eyes briefly swept the graceful writing, hiding the flood of relief at what it didn't say.

"Explain to me why my mother painted Peter Randall."

Chester Caughlin persevered as his mind journeyed to the night Jonas had called, the night before he died. His friend, so sad, so lost.

"You've known all along, haven't you Chet?" Jonas McCabe's voice on the phone did not sound angry or betrayed, only tired and weak.

Chester did not respond. His last hope of protecting his friend from the truth was lost. Somehow, Jonas had put the pieces together.

Standing on the stairs to the loft when he arrived, Jonas' face was pale. In his hand, an envelope yellowed with age. Across the room, Chester saw the desk covered with copies of old newspaper articles. His heart sank.

They talked until the wee hours of the morning.

"Why didn't she tell us?"

He watched as Jonas traced his rough calloused fingers over the words his daughter had written long ago. The handwriting, beautiful, had led Jonas to the frightening conclusion involving Maggie and the death of Peter Randall.

His lifelong friend knew there was no need to ask for Chester's silence. The retired sheriff had kept it for years.

Driving out the lane, Chester's rearview mirror flashed red as flames danced in the farm's burn barrel. He left, never revealing to Jonas the final piece of the puzzle. One to confirm the worst.

Well trained in interrogation, her intensity would have shaken even the most seasoned.

As he had rehearsed in anticipation of this day, he spoke. "What happened then had nothing to do with your mother, Jessica."

His blatant attempt to avoid her questions was serving to upset the troubled woman even more. He would address the portrait at some point. First, he must to diffuse the current situation.

"I wasn't supposed to find any of this, was I?"

Jessica's bluntness reminded Chester, she was a McCabe.

"The letter, the newspaper articles and the portrait all indicate a link between my mother and Peter Randall. Let me rephrase, the *death* of Peter Randall."

Chester pointed to the yellowed page. "Do you see Peter Randall's name in this?" By the grace of God, his name was absent.

"Did she kill him, Chester?"

Jonas' words exactly.

"Is my mother a murderer?"

Chester's commitment was undaunted. Nothing would be gained.

"Your mother was not involved in Peter Randall's death," Chester betrayed nothing. Speaking with the controlled authority he had years ago, surrounded by reporters.

"That's it!" Jessica's fist slammed the table. "Chester, you cannot dismiss this like I'm some child."

She picked up the article containing the photographs of a sheriff he barely recalled. "You were there and you're telling me--" She stopped. "You promised Jonas, didn't you Chester?"

"No Jessica." Her clench easing, he reclaimed the paper. "There is no promise because Maggie had nothing to do with Peter Randall's death."

"Then why the sudden interest in him, Chester...or had he always suspected this?"

"I won't lie to you, Jess. You're grandfather had suspicions over the years about who your father was." There could be no hint of doubt until he had all the bases covered.

"He went through stages where he thought he had the answer. The Randall boy's death was pure coincidence. And as your grandfather realized another dead end." He measured her for any sign of acceptance.

***

Patty Ann Conrad was in full fall cleaning mode, not her original plan for the day. Jessica's call asking for Steven had altered that.

Cleaning and organizing helped her to work through whatever was bothering her. Jessica's troubled voice was definitely bothering her.

On the step stool, she waved a broom covered with a towel at cobwebs that tried to dance out of her way.

"Mom."

Patty Ann's son rarely used this maternal endearment. His tone triggered unease.

"We have to talk about Uncle Peter."

Patty Ann stopped, met with a look that failed to hide the torment.

Down from the stool she followed her son into the kitchen.

***

Jessica left Chester Caughlin's disillusioned, angry and more determined than ever.

A block from Andrew's home her cell phone rang. An illegal u-turn had her in front of 862 Chestnut in record time.

Steven, on the front step, met her. "Hey." Frowning, he put an arm around her shoulders giving a brotherly squeeze. "Held good on your promise, hmm?"

"I've been to Chester's."

Steven stopped.

"He told me my mother had nothing to do with your uncle," she shoved her hands in her front pockets. "I want to believe him Steven, I..."

"Come in here, hon." Patty Ann Conrad held the screen door. "I think I can help."

The physical and mental exhaustion overtaking Jessica squelched the urge to scream as Steven's mother methodically moved about the kitchen. Placing the final cup on the table, next to a plate of freshly baked muffins, she perched on a seat.

"First, Chester is right," Patty Ann calmly continued. "Did you know your mother and I were best friends in college?"

She should have been shocked, yet another piece of her mother's life hidden. But, compared to what she had encountered so far, this was nothing.

"Our dorm room was always filled with canvases, brushes..." Patty Ann smiled. "I bet I sat in wet paint at least once a week that first year.

"Your mother would beg anyone to sit so she could paint them. Even my brother." She looked up at Jessica. "Your mother's painting of Peter has nothing more to do with you than any other portrait in that loft."

Jessica could feel Steven observing her.

"She was with me that night, Jessica."

A wave out of nowhere struck Jessica, and she watched as it reflected onto Patty Ann Conrad. Turmoil kept in check for the last 24 hours began to manifest, brimming at the edge of Jessica's lashes.

"We had kept in touch even after she dropped out of school, and I had come to visit her that weekend."

Patty Ann knelt in front of Jessica, taking the young

woman's face. "Chester Caughlin knows no more about how my brother died than you or I."

***

Chester descended the steps to the basement room where he kept all his gear from many years as a county sheriff.

He unlocked the gun cabinet and retrieved the box that until a month ago had not been touched in over 30 years.

The key in his hand was small and gold. As he unlocked the box and opened its lid, the horror of that day rushed at him as his eyes rested on the small broken locket, the envelope alongside it yellowed with age. His thumb tentatively rubbed the shiny locket's inscription.

Sheriff Chester Caughlin looked down into the ravine. Finding a body was not an everyday occurrence. He gingerly descended the steep hill of black Iowa dirt.

"Sheriff, do you see it?" the young deputy's question rolled over the edge of the ravine.

Chester didn't respond as he walked to the still figure. The early June morning had brought with it heavy dew. He moved cautiously.

The face pricked at a memory in his subconscious. Walking to the other side of the body, he saw the red ground behind the young man's head.

Chester slowly went over the scene. The marks on the ravine wall and the way the body laid one could deduce the young man had fallen. Or, been pushed.

Light touched on a shiny object clasped in the now stiff fingers. Chester bent closer. It was a locket, a broken locket, with an inscription.

"You finding anything, Sheriff?" The deputy's voice echoed, as he skidded down the hill to where his boss was standing.

Chester rose from his position near the lifeless form. "We better call Phil O'Connor..." He brushed his hands together. "Then we better check if anyone is missing around here." He turned and climbed up the hill.

Chester Caughlin closed the gun cabinet. Everything was back in its place and locked. He felt tired as he ascended the steps into the sun-filled kitchen and dialed the phone. It rang once.

"Hello, Doc Harrison."

CHAPTER 20

Jessica left Steven and his mother, much to Patty Ann's disapproval.

Steven hadn't argued.

The entire exchange was not quite right.

Arriving at the acreage, she went straight to the office.

She had rerun the childhood scene a thousand times. Dashing up the loft stairs that sunny summer day, she had come upon her grandfather standing on top of a tall step stool sliding a box to the back of the shelf. Startled, he registered an uncharacteristic panic.

It had come to her for a reason.

On the second shelf above the file cabinet, she groped blindly. Her fingertips came to a metal surface. It was not covered in a thick dust as were the rest of the loft's boxes and cabinets. Speculation gnawed.

Sitting on the floor, legs crossed in front of her, Jessica confronted the box. "Oh God, Jonas, I'm scared." She turned the key left in the lock.

Even though bright, the sunlight was somewhat lost in the great expanse of the barn's loft. At first, she wasn't quite sure what she was seeing.

Envelopes, held in a bundle by a rubber band.

Then, trapped in a shaft of light, the glint of a small gold object, a locket. Jessica knew who it belonged to.

She reached for the gleaming, fragile, heart-shaped pendant. Only half was there, hanging from its delicate golden chain. The front was gone. Turning it, her eyes fell upon the inscription scrolled eloquently across the inside.

"Forever J".

Tears blurred the golden heart, falling, landing on the box's contents.

She removed the rubber band encircling the envelopes. Written to Maggie McCabe, her name, though faded, appeared on the front. No return address, no sign of the author.

Jessica opened the first envelope and slid the contents into the dim light of the loft. The premonition seeped into her.

Love is what we make it, my dearest
Maggie.

Jessica stopped. Jonas had kept this from her for a reason. She began to shudder.

***

After leaving the bakery, Matthew drove aimlessly around Gracier furious with himself. *Why had he told Steven? Jessica deserved to hear this first!* He prayed Steven's devotion to Jessica would override his hatred for Matthew.

The sun was ascending to noon as he pulled into the McCabe family farm.

The loft door was open. He wasn't surprised.

She did not hear his entrance.

"Jess."

Matthew sank at the sight of the papers. By the sheer will of God, the single initial scribbled at the bottom of the page yielded nothing to her.

"Why would he keep this from me?"

She was thinking out loud, and Matthew hoped for some clue to what she did or didn't know. His gut told him Steven's overprotective nature towards Jessica had been Matthew's saving grace.

"Or is this what you're supposed to explain to me, Matthew?" She held up the remaining letters, and then a broken locket. She flipped it over.

He became transfixed on the initial etched in the gold. The questions were gone. What Jonas McCabe had told him was true.

Anger overtook Matthew, no longer clouded by the hope, rather completely focused on the hate he had for his father. Their father. And the abandonment of his daughter.

"Oh my God...oh my God." Jessica stood up, the papers fluttering to the ground.

Matthew caught her, afraid she would stumble. She jerked away. The dark secret he had tried to disprove had come out of the past, into the light.

"How long have you...?" She stopped. Her hands went to her temples. "How stupid could I be?"

The sound of her eerie laughter filled the room, making Matthew sick.

"You've got to listen to me." Matthew kept his distance as she paced the floor of the loft.

"Listen to you." Jessica halted mid step. "Listen to you!" The anger seized every inch of her body. "Get out of here."

"I'm not leaving until you hear all of this. Why Jonas did it this way."

"You're the voice on the phone that night."

He said nothing as the enlightenment grew.

"The voice, the land deal."

Matthew's silence held.

"How long had Jonas known?"

She was running the timeline...how, when, and most importantly why. He couldn't let it go any further.

"Ever since the night your mother died."

Jessica's pace slowed.

"I questioned at first why Jonas hadn't confronted him. Why he didn't demand what was rightfully yours." The reference to Joseph as their father was almost more than he could bear to say.

Jessica's head shook.

"But Joseph had abandoned you and your mother. In Jonas' mind, that severed all rights he had." Matthew fully expected her to leave at any moment, instead motionless, she stared blankly at the rough wooden walls.

"Why...you?"

"He had never planned on telling anyone..." Matthew's very being wrenched as it had the day Jonas had told him. "But he didn't plan on us falling in love."

Jessica bent over, hands on her knees.

"He came to me with all of this because he knew I would do anything for you. Even if it meant losing you forever." Matthew tried to restrain the shaking, "and he was right."

"When...when did he..."

"Remember, I went home early the weekend we were going to tell our families." Matthew's hands began to tremble as they had that day.

"I didn't believe Jonas at first, Jess. Then he showed me the things he had found over the years, including the letters." He nodded to the yellowed pieces of paper now lying in a pile on the floor of the loft.

"What does the land deal have to do with this?" Jessica's confusion and anger at being kept in the dark was in her voice and the rigid stance of her body.

"Jonas and I became close. And we both struggled with the secret we kept." Matthew ran his hand through his hair. "We argued about telling you. To Jonas it was a no-win situation. You'd want nothing from him and yet, would have to live with the knowledge that Joseph Cassidy is your father."

Jessica now on the far side of the room sat on a stack of boxes.

Matthew watched helpless as the hidden secrets took their toll. There was no turning back.

"It all changed the day I intercepted a call meant for my father, a call concerning the land deal." Matthew walked back and forth as if in a courtroom. He prayed she would understand the reasoning behind what he and Jonas had done. "I hoped it would be a way Jonas could find peace with all of this."

Matthew turned to her.

She didn't move.

"He could finally give to you what was rightfully yours and leave our father with the fate he deserved. Jonas did it to protect you and to right a horrible wrong."

"How does all this right a wrong, let alone justify your involvement?" Her fingertips rested on each temple. "Jonas has me owning land with my brother, a Cassidy..." She could barely speak the words. "And my father, who makes no claim to me, owns all the land around it."

"The land is my mother's."

Jessica's gaze rose from the floor of the loft.

"My father put it all in her name years ago. He had gotten into financial trouble." Matthew stopped, letting it sink in, the Land Corporation's truest purpose exposed.

"Does your mother know about me? About any of this?"

Her questions were those that had torn Matthew. His parents' relationship defied logic.

"I've never asked her," Matthew hushed.

"You can't leave her in the dark, Matthew."

Her compassion, even now, this woman he adored, still

selfless.

"He's hurt her so much over the years. She amazes me, in spite of everything..."

The room filled with a heaviness neither he nor Jessica seemed to be able to move under.

The sky had become clouded. Still the unusually hot October day was causing the air to become stifling, compressing Matthew's lungs, almost suffocating.

Jessica stood above the pile of letters strewn on the floor.

"I've always imagined her, an independent spirit, not afraid. But to love a man like Joseph Cassidy..."

Matthew wanted to take her in his arms, but couldn't.

He began to pick up the letters that had landed next to the cabinet. The familiar headlines leaped at him.

"Where did you get these?" Matthew raised the newspaper articles he now clenched.

"On the floor, between the wall and Jonas' desk."

Matthew could feel the blood drain.

***

The sound of Matthew's pickup had long since faded into the distance.

Up onto the stool, she placed the box on the shelf.

Peter Randall was not her father, clearing any doubt she had of her mother's involvement in his death. There should be relief. There was none.

CHAPTER 21

Jessica had a number of patients boarding, and the wind that rushed through the trees was beginning to rile them.

A wicked steel blue line of clouds raced across the sky as she shut the barn door. The wild-eyed animals conveyed the severity of the storm moving their way. Rare for late October, the weather report's prediction of severe thunderstorms by the afternoon appeared right on track. Despite the world she knew crashing around her, she had a lot to get done.

***

Joseph Cassidy relaxed behind the dark expanse of his mahogany desk, its top polished to a glossy finish. The storm brewing in the sky outside his window cast an ominous reflection.

He had spared no expense, his surroundings, nothing but the best. A leader, envied by many in this small Midwestern town, his image in the community, unprecedented. He reveled in it. Whatever he set his sights on he got, one way or another.

The clap of thunder coincided with his office door swinging wide, his reaction cut short by his son's entrance into the room.

"Good afternoon, Matthew." He tilted back in his chair, in control. He prided himself on it. "This is an unexpected visit."

Matthew displayed more than the usual contempt.

Matthew didn't speak as he placed a piece of paper on the desk. Peter Randall, frozen in time, lay before him.

His nonchalant gaze, second nature, a master at evading responsibility for anything that might tarnish his pristine image.

Why, he'd even convinced the locals he was totally unaware of the real reason behind the land deal that had failed. The concerned furrowed brow forced for the photographers the day the story broke about the land 'saved from developers' and his quote for the papers classic Cassidy.

"We are grateful to the Lancaster County Land Corporation and its vision of keeping our land safe for future generations."

With this signature cool composure, he picked up the worn copy in his well-manicured hands.

"You amaze me."

Matthew's usual disdain verged on rage, a hatred Joseph had not heard before.

How could he have had such a son? Pathetic, bleeding heart. Definitely, a product of his mother's doting.

"How do you do it? How do you live a life void of emotion?" Matthew leaned across the desk. "How can I be your son?"

"Yes, you are my son. But don't think I haven't asked myself the same." The papers, back on the desk, he slid them to Matthew who towered over him.

"Matthew, I don't know where you're coming from on this one?" He gestured half-heartedly at the articles.

Finished with the conversation, Joseph stood up. "You could use a glass or two of this. May I pour you some?" In front of the cherry wood liquor cabinet, Joseph reached for the crystal decanter filled with his favorite bourbon.

Matthew's glare fixed on Joseph.

"I've seen the letters," Matthew's voice, a low rumble, a warning thunder, rolled from a faraway horizon.

Joseph filled a heavy crystal tumbler, his aloof manner serving to infuriate his son. He relished the power, able to control people simply by not reacting.

Matthew, at the door, stopped. "I've seen the locket. She knows. She knows it all."

His son came at him defying the boundaries that had defined their relationship.

"Take a look around because your world is about to end."

For one brief moment, he saw in the young man's eyes the person his son loathed.

A sliver of fear sliced a hairline fracture in his infamous

impenetrable facade.

The door closed as the crystal tumbler exploded at is feet on the imported marble tile.

***

The clouds churned above his head as he approached the barn. He entered unannounced. The wind howled up the loft opening.

She descended the stairs, a box tucked under her arm, to see him closing the office door.

"You're confused." Jessica crossed to the desk. "You're not welcome here."

Joseph appraised the girl he had observed at a distance for years. He wanted to fulfill the fantasy, to see however brief, a hint of himself in her. Her defiant beauty was entirely Maggie's.

He fixed on the locket in her hand.

"Your mother, I wager to say, would not have agreed with you."

Jessica whirled on her heel. The anger and disgust confirmed whose daughter she was.

Jessica yanked open the office door. "Leave, *now*."

Debris flew through the farmyard. Inside the office, there was no acknowledgment of the world outside.

"You can't stand the thought, can you?" Joseph walked to the desk, taking a seat in the worn leather chair. The locket lay on the desk beside. "The world was a lot different then, Jessica."

He nonchalantly surveyed the desk and the articles it contained, covering Peter Randall's mysterious death. He resolved to end this once and for all.

His eyes locked on the yellowed paper in her hand...*the letter.*

There she was, Maggie, the letter, begging. Humiliation buried, where no one was allowed, now stripped clean. The anger renewed.

"We were in love."

The void seen in Maggie's eyes, now in hers, was all he needed.

"But your mother made one unforgivable mistake." He met the fiery stare of the young woman. "I'm a married man."

Jessica's mind reeled. In all she'd dealt with, it had not occurred to her. Had that been the real reason for all the lies and secrets, the shame?

He spoke to her thoughts.

"Maria and I were separated, although few people knew it."

Joseph's demeanor, a metamorphosis, rippled across his features, a snake shedding his skin.

"We were all at the University then." He looked at her. "Gracier was miles away. It provided the anonymity."

"Why you?"

Joseph flushed hot at her implication.

"You're just like your mother." He flew up, the locket clenched in his fist. "That 'holier than thou' attitude."

Jessica watched the gold heart dangle precariously between his white knuckled grip.

"Well, I was good enough for her once."

Jessica's skin crawled.

"What does Peter Randall have to do with all this?"

Joseph Cassidy was suddenly quiet. An air came over him.

"She didn't mean to kill Peter." He fingered the locket, his features like stone. "It was an accident." An uneven redness climbed his neck into his clean-shaven jaw. Muscles flinched. "She thought she was in love with him. She thought she could convince him. But he would never love her...like I do."

Nausea overcame Jessica at the present tense he used. She gagged on the bile that burned the back of her throat.

***

Matthew turned the corner as the tornado touched down on the dirt road bordering the McCabe farm.

The scanner had gone off as he sat across the table from Steven, a last hope of someone who might get through to her. The sirens stopped neither from running to the truck.

He began to quake uncontrollably as the twister cherry picked the buildings, exploding each into splinters, drawing them up into its white funnel.

Time came to a halt, both imprisoned in the surreal horror. *Dear God don't—*

The red Jeep flying into the air stopped his lament cold.

The twister moved ominously into the black furrowed field, and the revolving white became dark gray as it filled with the rich Iowa soil.

Livestock from the neighboring farms: pigs, cows and

pieces of grain silos sucked up into the darkness. Then tired of playing, the twister threw them to the ground to land in a contorted broken heap.

As if a switch thrown, the tornado ascended leaving the earth on which it had danced its terrifying waltz. The sun lit up his rearview mirror.

Matthew rammed the truck into gear, gravel spun under the wheels.

Pieces of timber, twisted metal and dead farm animals littered the farmyard and covered the pasture.

The barn where Jonas and now Jessica had her office and the white farmhouse were the only buildings left standing.

Shattered glass covered the lawn. Except for the panes in the front door, gaping holes were all that remained of the home's windows.

Matthew stopped the pickup and ran for the back door. He felt Steven on his arm. He turned, his heart in his throat.

His father's black Lincoln sat parked outside the office. A large maple crushed the leather top down the middle of the vehicle.

Shouting her name, they ran towards the barn. Steven reached the door first. Matthew, noting it wasn't about to budge, crawled through the hole that used to be the office window.

Harvey raised his head.

Matthew could see her hand next to the faithful dog's paws, perfectly still.

"Jess!" Panic threatened to overtake. The glass sliced his

clothing, tearing at his legs and arms as Matthew squeezed under the mangled timbers of the building. His fingers pressed her wrist. "She has a pulse, Steven!"

Matthew assessed the debris on top of Jessica. The desk bore the weight of the office roof that hovered precariously over her.

Steven, now next to Matthew, pointed above his head, "If I can lift this we can slide her out." Steven leaned into the timbers and pushed.

Matthew rammed the office chair under to give some support.

As the men hoisted the expanse of wood, Matthew saw the blood soaking Jessica's side.

"My God." Steven instantly paled. "We've got to get her out now!"

Matthew slid his arms carefully under Jessica's shoulders and began to drag her out from under the dark cavern of wood. The moan from her limp body seized him. *Hold on, Jess. Hold on.*

As he carried her out the door, Matthew saw his father underneath the loft stairs. The locket clenched in his grasp caught the rays of sunlight, shining from above, where the office roof used to be.

Steven made his way to where Joseph Cassidy's body lay, crushed beyond recognition. His fingers paused briefly on his wrist.

Matthew continued on to the truck.

Steven fell in behind.

Matthew knew his father had not survived.

"I've seen injuries like Jess's before, Matthew."

Matthew couldn't take his eyes off the woman in his arms. He didn't doubt Steven. He'd seen the photojournalist's work over the years, the pictures he'd taken and the violent world observed through his well-traveled camera lens.

"We've got to get her to the hospital, but first we need Andrew."

***

Doctor Andrew Harrison had lived in Iowa his entire life and he had not seen a storm like this, let alone in October.

He opened the door to survey the damage. The oak where his children's tree house had resided for 50 years now laid toppled, its giant, gnarled roots exposed. The rusted swing set stood to the side of the entangled limbs, missed by a matter of inches.

He turned at the sound of the truck as it stopped in the street.

Steven jumped out from behind the wheel.

Something was terribly wrong.

"Get your bag, Andrew!"

He went straight into the house, back within a matter of moments.

As he neared the truck, he saw Matthew sitting in the passenger seat cradling Jessica, his arms and legs covered in blood. His shirt, pressed against a gash in her side, soaked to a dark crimson.

"Steven, get the Eldorado."

Steven ran to the garage.

Andrew, having acted quickly to check her vital signs and the gaping wound, looked into Matthew's horrified face.

Steven beside the pickup threw the Cadillac into park and jumped out.

"Take this, Steven."

Working together, Andrew and Matthew transferred Jessica into the back seat.

She whimpered as they laid her in the vehicle.

Matthew crawled in and gently positioned her head in his lap.

Andrew climbed into the back. Steven shut the door and jumped in behind the steering wheel.

"St. Joseph's, Steven, as fast as you can." *Oh, child. I can't handle another... If you ever needed to be stubborn, it's now.* His hands moved deftly over her.

Your chance of making it to heaven was a long shot old man, but if you're there. Andrew swallowed, his composure was essential.

The rearview mirror reflected Steven's distress.

Andrew returned his attention to Matthew. The young lawyer's lips parted in prayer as he stroked her hair.

"The phones are dead. There's no way to call ahead." Andrew rifled through his bag. "It was on the scanner, the ambulance was destroyed, the fire station collapsed."

Andrew grabbed the handle of the car door as Steven swerved to miss the debris that littered the streets.

Careening onto the highway, Andrew watched helpless as Jessica's hand clenched into a fist, her knuckles marbling red to white.

Then in a rasping whisper came the same words Maggie had spoken that fateful night, "Not you Joseph, not you."

CHAPTER 22

Matthew stood in the hallway, the smell of the hospital invading him. Steven leaned against the wall on the other side of the doorway.

Upon arrival, hospital staff rushed Jessica into the emergency room. The two men found the wait intolerable.

The door swung open and Andrew, sleeves rolled up, donning scrubs covered in blood, emerged.

The world around Matthew began to crumble.

"We've got her stable. She required a few stitches to say the least. Her spleen may be damaged. We'll know more in a few hours." He pulled off his surgical cap. "There's a more immediate problem. She's lost a lot of blood, and her blood type is rare and in short supply."

"I might be able to help." Matthew's promise had come to an end.

"Get your mother here, Steven."

Steven registered shock.

"Andrew?" Matthew was at a loss. "She's my--"

"Now!"

Steven headed for the nurses' station as Andrew barked orders after him.

"Tell them to get a hold of the sheriff's department. They'll send a car out to get her." Stopping, he turned to Matthew. "Son, you better get in touch with your mother."

Dread landed, a fist in Matthew's abdomen, his mother had no idea that her husband was dead.

***

The patrol car pulled up in front of St. Joseph's Hospital.

Matthew watched as Steven, anxiously awaiting his mother's arrival, strode out the hospital doors.

Andrew met mother and son at the entry to the unit where Jessica was resting. No one had been permitted, and wouldn't be, until Andrew knew she could tolerate it.

Placing an arm on Patty Ann Conrad's shoulder, he spoke. Only she could hear. They disappeared inside.

Matthew's mind flashed to his mother. Chester would be there by now. Matthew had decided to contact the Sheriff's department asking them to forward his message to their former boss. The news of Joseph's death, delivered by Chester would be easier on her. The sadness he felt was for her alone.

"Steven, Matthew," Chester Caughlin came from behind, "we got here as quick as we could."

Maria Cassidy walked up the hallway to her son.

"She insisted on coming." Chester nodded towards Matthew's mother. "There was no discussing it."

"How is she doing?"

Matthew wasn't shocked by her compassion for Jessica or her calm resolve in the matter of her husband's death. She had lost him long ago.

"Her spleen may have been damaged. She's pretty beat up. " Matthew struggled, trying to collect the pieces, to put them in order. Nothing came, except the thought of losing her. "She's lost a lot of blood..."

"They say she's stable." Steven was standing outside the door to the room where his mother was now giving blood.

Chester approached Matthew and Maria. "You have my sympathies." Hat in hand, he continued, "Joseph has been moved to O'Connor's."

Matthew looked at his mother, then to the retired Sheriff. "Thank you, Chester."

Doctor Andrew Harrison came through the door, a grin spread across his well-earned furrows. "She's awake. And damn if she isn't just like him." Shaking his head, he chuckled. "She wanted to know if the animals were okay."

"Can we go in?" Matthew motioned to the door behind Andrew.

"First we need to discuss what's gone on here today."

Chester, sitting next to Maria, rose.

The group followed the old doctor into a small waiting room.

***

She tried to focus.

"Honey, don't try to move. Just relax."

Patty Ann's fingers traced just above her eyebrows.

Jessica's tongue breached the parched edges of her

mouth. She had no concept of time.

"Where's Steven?" Whatever they had given Jessica kept her just beyond the brink of consciousness. A nurse moved about the room.

Patty Ann spoke to the attendant, "Will you stay in the room with her?"

Jessica gave in, her eyes closed. She heard the door shut behind Steven's mother.

Steven immediately noticed his mother's tear streaked face. His stomach dropped.

"She's asking for Steven."

Steven was out the door, Andrew's approval a moot point.

"Okay Dorothy, we're not in Kansas anymore." Steven's sarcastic remark was successful as a smile parted her lips. She was deathly pale. He resolved to stay lighthearted.

"Joseph," her voice was so fragile, "Joseph Cassidy, Steven." Agony ran down her white cheeks.

Steven knelt beside the bed. She had no idea the barn had collapsed, no clue who had given her the life saving blood or the significance of the biological link.

"It can't be..."

"Don't, Jess." He wished the drugs running through her beaten and bruised body would numb her to more than the physical hurt.

"She needs to rest Steven." Andrew had quietly entered the room.

Steven didn't move at first.

Jessica began to drift off.

"How do we tell her, Andrew?"

Andrew opened the door. Reluctant, Steven succumbed to the invitation to leave.

"She has no idea your mother gave her blood does she?"

Steven shook his head.

"And we will leave it that way until she is ready to hear all of this."

This was an order, not a question. Steven didn't argue. The revelation was more than she would be able to handle now, if ever.

"I think it's best if we only go through this once."

Matthew stood looking out the window as Andrew and Steven rejoined the group.

"She has no idea." Steven's observation prompted little reaction.

Matthew left.

No one was by the door as he slipped into her room. "Dear God, please." Matthew gulped at the ache. There was no other way. He would...no, he *had* to let her go. The burden of the lie would be worth saving her from the tragedy.

Her hand, wet with his loss, didn't move.

***

Jessica awoke to the sun rising in the east. A hot knife shot into her side. Morphine would be her only reprieve. But she was not comfortable with the state it had put her in.

Some cold water sounded good. Reaching for the glass

of water at her bedside, the full spectrum of her injuries hit.

Losing her balance, the cup and pitcher of water crashed to the ground.

The door to the room burst, slamming against the wall. Jessica instinctively curled up into a ball on the floor as the blood pulsed in her abdomen.

Matthew was there. "Jess, are you all right?"

He lifted her onto the hospital bed.

"Doc Harrison will have your hide." The silver haired nurse not far behind clucked her tongue in warning.

Jessica held still as the attentive caregiver checked her IVs.

"What in the hell do you think you're doing, young lady?" Doctor Andrew Harrison had arrived.

"Your butt is in this bed until I say different." He situated his stethoscope in his ears.

She was too tired to argue.

Matthew stepped out of Andrew's way.

"Matthew, please leave the room while I examine her more thoroughly. No one comes in here until I give the okay. And that goes for Steven too."

Jessica said nothing as Matthew left the room.

Andrew sat on the bed beside her.

Worn out, in pain, she still had no problem recognizing the apprehension. He wrapped her hand inside his.

"Andrew," Jessica's voice was weak, "I'm afraid to know what part is the terrible nightmare and what part is real." She turned to the window, blinking furiously at the tidal wave, just on the brink.

"He told me. My...father told me." She captured a gulp of air. "He said he kept the secret to protect her memory...to protect me."

Jessica met the sorrowful eyes of Doctor Andrew Harrison. "He told me that my mother murdered Peter Randall." Sobbing, she gasped at the pressure in her chest.

"Honey, you--"

"No more lies Andrew...no more..." The medication he put into her IV was taking hold. Unwillingly, the battle to fight its effects over, she floated into a deep sleep.

CHAPTER 23

Jessica was sound asleep.

"It's time, Michael." Andrew's use of Mickey's given name reaffirmed the weight Maggie's childhood friend had carried on his shoulders.

"If I didn't know better, I'd swear it was her." Mickey, big hands shoved in his pockets shifted, one foot to the other. He was out of his element.

Andrew held the door wide.

Andrew followed Mickey Hansen's massive figure into the waiting room that was becoming smaller by the minute. It was presumed by all present that the local bar owner and longtime family friend had simply come to visit Jessica.

"Hey, Mick." Steven extended a hand.

Matthew turned from the window.

Patty Ann moved through the room, pouring coffee.

Andrew understood it eased her anxiety. Shortly, the routine would not suffice.

"I'll be outside." Maria Cassidy squeezed Patty Ann Conrad's arm.

"Maria, stay."

She obeyed Andrew's request, going back to the table.

Andrew looked around the room. "I promised Jonas I'd do it his way." He stopped at Chester. "And now we're all going to."

The entire room stood silent.

"Jonas McCabe believed without question that Joseph Cassidy was Jessica's father." Andrew sat adjacent to Maria.

Her face portrayed nothing.

"And I believed it too, for two reasons."

On cue, Steven pulled the locket from his coat pocket. "This was in Joseph's ..." Steven stopped. "We found it in the office with them." He placed it on the table in front of Andrew.

The "J" inscribed inside the shiny gold locket seemed to leap from the past.

"She wore that locket around her neck until the night she died. Joseph Cassidy's name was the last she spoke." His hand rested a top the small woman's folded grasp. "Forgive me, Maria."

"Jonas had little doubt. The more he found, the more it led to the same conclusion. He waited for Joseph to step forward as the father. That dreaded day never came." Andrew looked in the direction of Mickey Hansen.

"Maggie came to me that night. She had gotten a call. Peter was coming to see her. She was distraught, but agreed to meet, scared to death he would show up at the farm."

Mickey looked across the room to Patty Ann. "I had figured out months before that Peter was the father. I swore to her I'd never tell."

Andrew recognized anger on the Irishman.

"I told her it was a damn stupid idea to involve Joseph, but she had her mind set on keeping the truth from Peter. He saw it as his chance to..." Mickey Hanson's mouth bent with a sneer, a contempt for Joseph Cassidy. "He took advantage of the situation and almost got exactly what he always wanted."

The towering figure seemed torn. "It was several hours later, I was at the bar closing up. Dad had left for home. I was alone. Maggie showed up a little after 2:00 a.m. She was crying hysterically, pointing at the locket, and that's when I saw the red welt on her neck." Mickey gestured to the gold necklace lying on the table. "She kept repeating how angry he had been and how he had tried to rip it off her neck." He paused. "She went into labor. I called Jonas and Ann."

Andrew studied Matthew as he turned, first to his mother, then to Andrew.

Mickey's voice was thick. "She was terrified and kept saying how it had all gone terribly wrong." He stopped.

Andrew wasn't sure if Mickey would be able to finish.

"The next day they..." Mickey's expression contorted.

The bear of a man was trembling.

"Maggie McCabe was my best friend," the passion and loyalty was unmistakable. "I knew her better than anyone. She did not kill Peter Randall." His fierce devotion was undeniable. "It was a horrible accident!"

Patty Ann sank into a chair. The carafe holding the coffee slid from her hand. Steaming hot liquid pooled around her feet.

Steven, immediately at her side, wiped the hot liquid, patting her skin. There was no cry.

"So you two knew this?" Steven stunned, seemed to choke on his anger. "What in the hell we're you planning on doing when she found out?"

"Oh Lord. What did I do?" Patty Ann broken, wept.

"We weren't going to let her find out," Chester's voice was low and controlled.

"Not let her find out!" Steven was beginning to grow hostile. "Didn't you consider once she saw all Jonas had left behind--"

"He didn't leave them for her to find. And none of us had any idea what the other thought they knew or had promised Jonas." Andrew took in Steven and Matthew. "Chester called me after Jessica confronted him with the letter and articles. We then realized Jonas' final discovery had told a truth about Maggie worse than anything he could have ever imagined." He glanced at Mickey. "Mickey brought Maggie to the hospital that night. We knew he had seen or heard something for her to go to him."

"When did he find the letter? How long had he suspected she was involved in Peter Randall's death?"

Andrew's heart went out to Matthew and the turmoil he had contained to honor his promise to Jonas.

"Jonas exhausted every scenario. It was not a matter of denial. To admit to it would have revealed the terrible facts we are dealing with now." Chester acknowledged Andrew. "It was something we were all willing to live with."

"Mom, why didn't you tell me?" Steven's voice could not hide his disillusion.

Andrew had struggled with the details he should divulge to Steven's mother. He still had reservations about his decision.

Patty Ann's color drained. "From what Maggie had told me that night...I...I held on to the hope that my brother's death..." Patty Ann Conrad locked on Chester Caughlin's bowed head. Then, as if turning a page in a book, she began to recall the night of her brother's death.

"I decided to visit her that weekend, the weekend Jessica was born. I was supposed to go home to Earlton.

"Maggie had sounded so sad over the phone." Patty Ann's expression traveled across the years. "I called Peter and told him so he could head home without me. I told him that Maggie was pregnant...," she faltered. "I hadn't said anything to anyone until then because she had begged me not to. She wanted it kept quiet. It was for reasons I had never imagined."

Andrew watched Steven, uneasy.

"Maggie was surprised, glad even to see me." Patty Ann betrayed a moment of happiness.

"Despite the circumstances something told me she was okay, content with the baby. I asked her again why she refused to tell the father." Patty Ann's voice was all but there, "I had no idea."

It was clear Patty Ann Conrad ran the scene through her

mind, one she had not wanted to relive.

"Someone called late that afternoon, shortly after I arrived. She was crying when she returned to the room but convinced me she was just an overly emotional, pregnant woman." Patty Ann blinked fiercely. "I'm certain now that it was Peter." She gathered herself.

"Then suddenly she started talking about things that until then I don't think she had any intention of doing. It was all to protect Peter. I was so blind." She did not hide the shame and embarrassment at her ignorance.

"No one knew about their relationship," Mickey's low baritone reverberated throughout the room. "They had gone to a lot of trouble to keep it that way."

"Maggie showed me the locket that night. She told me the father was a married man and she was not going to ruin a marriage." Patty Ann lowered her eyes. "She told me to insure I would be convinced it was someone I did not know. And she did a good job."

Memories, well hidden, flickered across her face.

"Sitting on the front porch later that evening, Joseph drove in. I knew him from college." Patty Ann paused. "It was after she had the baby and I thought back on that night...I was positive I had solved who the baby's father was and why she would not give in to such a man being a part of her child's life."

Andrew followed Patty Ann's gaze, the recipient, Maria Cassidy, unaffected.

"I left that evening to head for home. When Jonas called the next day to tell me Maggie had died, I decided then the secret would die with her."

She fixed on Steven, searching, Andrew suspected, for forgiveness.

Andrew prayed she would receive it.

"I believed it until you showed me the letter. The one Maggie had written..." Patty Ann's voice fell away. "The unsigned letters and poems we found among his belongings, they were Maggie's."

She looked out the window. "We received the call early Sunday morning. I...I blamed myself for the accident. I assumed Peter had misunderstood my message and driven to Gracier to pick me up." Her softly creped hand pressed to her face. "And it was because of me, but for a much different reason."

"Why?" Steven implored her. "Why would you want her to live with the belief that Joseph Cassidy was her father?"

"Because I was afraid it was true. That Maggie had killed Peter." Her eyes pleaded. "Thirty years of unspoken blame...hidden suspicions. It was enough."

Steven, arms now around his mother, began to rock her.

A lifetime of purgatory. And it was far from over.

"What in God's name do we tell her?" Steven, comforting his mother, stood up his blatant anger darting between the two old men. It was obvious who he held responsible for keeping the secret well hidden.

"Is it better to think your father is Joseph Cassidy?" Matthew turned to the window. "Or that your mother murdered your father?"

***

The door to the waiting room flew open. Everyone jumped.

"Doc!"

Matthew and Steven were right behind Andrew as he ran the length of the hall. "You two stay here!" He disappeared into her room.

Back out within a few short minutes, Andrew fired orders at the nurse. "Get Dr. Lois in here pronto. We're gonna have to take care of this spleen."

Andrew kept his voice level, "Steven, get your mother. We may need more blood and yours too, if it's a match."

Steven nodded.

"Matthew, she's calling for you, but by God if you upset her, I'll kick your attorney's--"

Matthew was around Andrew and into the room before another warning could be leveled.

"You must be Matthew." The nurse finished checking vitals and left the room.

Slipping up beside Jessica, Matthew hesitated at taking her hand.

"Matthew."

He started to respond, but stopped. His name crossed her beautiful lips, absently, as she wavered in and out of consciousness.

"Matthew."

He let himself become enraptured with her beauty. He'd been right. However, the affirmation was hollow.

Her eyes opened. "You loved me."

A peace settled over her, the alarms surreal.

Andrew pushed Matthew to the side. Steven burst through the door, a team of hospital staff on his heels.

"I can't lose you again. Don't die... don't die..." Matthew watched powerless as the medical team rushed around the room.

"Okay, we've got her, Doc." The young doctor assisting spoke to Andrew. "Doctor Lois is on his way."

"Matthew."

Steven gripped his shoulder.

"She's going to be okay, Matthew. She has to be."

"Everybody get out of this room!" Doctor Harrison's command left no room for debate. "Steven, go with Dr. Bennet and get ready."

Matthew stared at the ashen face of the woman he loved more than life itself. He was not leaving.

CHAPTER 24

It felt good to sit up and not have the pain shoot unrelenting. A bright blue autumn sky filled the world outside her window. Leaves clung tightly to a red oak just beyond, not eager to admit another Iowa winter was around the corner.

A week had gone by since her emergency surgery. The numbing throb of injuries replaced with the harsh reality of questions that had haunted her as she drifted in and out of consciousness. The fantasy of Maggie McCabe, young, unwed mother, stood in stark contrast.

"Hey, sleepy," Steven interrupted low and quiet.

She blinked at the tears that pressed her lashes. He pretended not to see.

"Snow White and Sleeping Beauty have nothing on you."

Jessica squeezed Steven's hand. "Where's Andrew?"

Steven pulled a chair up to the bed. "The nurse paged Doc when she saw your light. I decided I would sneak in without permission." He smiled at the blatant defiance of the good doctor's orders. "You scared us half to death, young lady."

Jessica was in no mood for games. "He's my brother, Steven." The final loss of Matthew, the reality of what had happened, nothing was left of her world.

No shock. No surprise. It was unnerving.

"But there's more, isn't there?"

Steven attempted his poker face. No wonder he lost his shirt at cards.

"Honey, I'll be right back." He winked. "Don't go anywhere."

"Steven!"

He was out the door.

***

Andrew, responding to the page, walked down the hallway to the room. He had been meeting with the surgeon to review what Jessica could handle.

The sight of Matthew and Steven in a heated exchange with Chester Caughlin greeted him. Both had been questioning what they'd heard and seen.

Regardless, he and Chester were determined to keep the last piece of the puzzle from her. Its implication would only add to the frightening speculation of how Peter Randall died.

"Damn it Chester, you think she won't demand more proof?" Steven seethed. "You think Jonas challenged what he uncovered? She'll be ten times worse, and she's got to live with it." Steven turned to the old sheriff. "What makes you so sure it was Maggie? And don't give me that BS 'it's a gut feeling'. I don't buy it."

Andrew stepped between the three men.

Maria and Patty Ann approached. They too had heard the altercation.

Oddly, the decades of betrayal exposed had caused a friendship to develop between the two women.

Matthew combed his hand through his hair. "Before we go in there, we better be on the same damn page with our story."

Silence prevailed.

The burden about to be put on the woman inside the hospital room was beyond comprehension.

Without warning, Chester pulled a small box from his pocket and lifted the lid.

From inside his coat pocket Andrew removed the broken locket and chain found in the loft. The two halves, separated for over 30 years, revealed themselves to one another. No one uttered a sound, upon seeing the small golden locket's inscription.

"To My Maggie...Forever J"

"This half of the locket was in Peter's hand that morning." The seasoned officer did not take his eyes off the pieces of broken jewelry. "I got the call early that morning on my way out to the ravine. She had taken a turn for the worse." His voice resonated, grave. "When she died that morning, I locked it away...I locked *all* of it away."

The two younger men didn't move.

"Chester never knew the other half of the inscription,"

Andrew's tone hushed. "Neither of us had any idea what the other kept hidden."

The nurse behind the station responded as the buzzer sounded next to Jessica's room number.

The conversation came to a standstill, until the nurse closed the door to Jessica's hospital room.

Reappearing, she gave a directive. "She is asking for Mr. Cassidy and Dr. Harrison."

Andrew looked at Matthew and then to Steven.

Receiving no argument, the two started to the door.

"Matthew," Maria Cassidy's voice caused both men to turn from the doorway.

Andrew found Maria's eyes and anguish.

The nurse closed the door to Jessica's room.

***

She was done waiting. Jessica reached for the call button, her thumb ready to press. Matthew and Andrew entered.

She could barely stand the sight of him.

"Jess," he hesitated, frightened.

She nodded as control dared to elude her.

He touched her pale cheek.

"Please, Matthew." She pushed him away. "I... I can't do this. There's something I --"

Andrew Harrison walked to the other side of the bed. "Honey, I was a fool. But I love you like one of my own, and I couldn't bear the thought..."

The kindhearted soul mirrored the torture she felt.

"Your grandfather was right, except for one thing."

Chester entered with Maria Cassidy.

Her manner, as always, composed. Raven black hair in short waves framed delicate porcelain that glowed.

Maria took a seat in the chair next to the bed.

The door opened again. It was Steven and Patty Ann.

A cold permeated Jessica like never before. The faces assembled were impossible to read.

"Jessica," Maria's voice was resolute, "Joseph is not your father."

The sobs that escaped racked Jessica's body.

Maria, without a moment's hesitation, enfolded Jessica's hand in hers. "He told you some terrible lies, a delusion he wanted to be true."

Joseph Cassidy rang through Jessica's head, *"She didn't mean to kill Peter...it was an accident."*

Jessica's teeth clenched against more than physical pain, "Where is he?"

"He's gone." No grief materialized.

"He told me my mother killed Peter Randall." She began to tremble.

Matthew was again at Jessica's side.

She chose the consolation of Maria. "He told me it was an accident. That she didn't mean to kill..."

"Damn it, Andrew, this is--"

Andrew silenced Steven.

"You have to listen to me, Jessica." Maria stroked the hair from Jessica's eyes.

She fell on to the pillow, gasping for air between the waves.

"Hon, let's take the edge off."

Jessica clutched Andrew's arm as he reached for the call button. "No...No medication."

Andrew stopped.

Standing up, Maria Cassidy stayed by Jessica. "Joseph and I had been separated for not quite a year."

It was evident Matthew was oblivious to this chapter from his parents' sordid life.

"Joseph stopped by on occasion, but had made it clear...they were in love, and I had resolved myself to the fact that he finally had the woman he'd wanted all his life." Maria hesitated. "However, things were not what they seemed."

Maria's eyes went around the room coming full circle to Jessica. "Your mother Maggie did not kill Peter Randall."

The room demonstrated no reaction.

"It had always been Maggie. I lived with it willingly." Her expression solemn, eased. "I couldn't hate her. She had no idea what his true motive was. She was deeply in love with another man, your father." Maria shook her head. "Now it's clear, to Joseph, the illusion had become all too real."

The small-framed woman bowed her head as Doctor Andrew Harrison and retired Sheriff Chester Caughlin stepped forward. Reaching into their respective pants pockets, they carefully placed two locket halves in Maria Cassidy's small hand.

"Thirty years ago I saw this locket. Foolish, I believed it was for me." Frail in stature, Maria Cassidy seemed anything but as she spoke her conclusion. "This locket speaks to what really happened."

Jessica's eyes froze on the words written inside the two broken halves.

"To My Maggie...Forever J"

It was too much.

"He came home unexpectedly. I heard the shower and got up. I saw it lying beside his keys, the broken half, and I prayed he was home for good."

Jessica looked at the inscription again.

"I had gotten back into bed and the phone rang. It was after 3:00 a.m. A young man's voice asked for Joseph. He was furious after taking the call." Maria stopped, her attention going briefly to Andrew and Chester. "I heard the car. My prayers had gone unanswered."

Jessica watched as Maria Cassidy became engulfed in the memory.

"The next morning he was at the kitchen table, radio on, drinking a cup of coffee." She paused.

"I didn't ask why he decided to come home. What mattered was my son would have a father." She twisted the diamond-encrusted wedding band, its opulence a testament to the façade of their marriage. "That would not be the last time I was wrong about Joseph Cassidy.

"Later that morning we heard Maggie McCabe had died. Joseph's response when he heard the news now makes perfect sense." Her voice fell, "'they both got what they deserved.'" Her dark eyes clouded. "I assumed he meant Maggie and the baby she'd left behind."

Maria's expression commanded belief. "I did not know who your father was. But, I knew who he wasn't. Joseph realized that night he would never have her."

Maria's voice was one of absolute certainty, unwavering. "The young man on the phone was Peter. And the last person to see him alive, the person who left the broken half with Peter, set it up to look as if Maggie had killed him. If Joseph couldn't have her, no one would."

"How...do you know all this?" Jessica faltered, shaken. And the other half of the locket, where--"

"Peter had it in is his hand the morning we found him. And she was gone." Chester looked to Jessica, receiving the understanding of his unstated decision.

Again, Jessica halted as she began to speak. She didn't care. "Why...why would she keep my father from knowing?"

Jessica met the gaze of her aunt.

"He had decided to become a priest." Patty Ann drew a ragged breath. "I don't believe Peter ever knew, Jess. Until his sister went to visit a friend...your mother."

Jessica was reminded of how deep the deception went.

"Why would Joseph want to convince Jessica that he was her father?" Steven directed his confusion at Maria.

The anger at what his father had done lingered in Matthew's voice. "I threatened him. And there it was, the perfect opportunity. He could once and for all prove to Jess that Maggie had done it. Joseph Cassidy would be the long lost suffering father, protecting her from the so-called truth."

"He would finally possess a part of her."

Jessica had not noticed Mickey until now.

His conviction resonated, "Maria's right. Joseph had been obsessed with Maggie for as long as I can remember. But to your mother they were nothing more than friends."

Mickey suddenly stopped. Then, his words, a revelation, addressed Maria. "She told me Joseph was furious about her meeting Peter that night..."

"That's when he must have tried to rip it from her neck," Maria finished Mickey's train of thought.

"Jess, when you came the other day I knew unless we did something you wouldn't give up. So, I called Andrew." Chester glanced at the old doctor. "The locket I believed Peter had given to Maggie was not that at all."

Jessica felt herself losing the battle.

Andrew moved bedside, eyeing her vitals. "We need to give her a break." He adjusted her pillows.

"Andrew, please, I've got to--"

"Your mother delivered at 3:00 a.m. that night." Andrew's gray whiskers, unshaven, glistened with his own relief. "You see, Maggie's little girl is proof of her innocence."

It swept across Jessica. Innocent, her mother was innocent.

"Everyone, you heard me." Andrew reverted to the habit of checking her pulse, allowing him to recover.

Mickey took charge of the door for the emotionally drained group.

Maria Cassidy stood.

Jessica caught her hand. "I'm sorry."

Patty Ann patted Jessica's arm. "I'll answer any

questions as best as I can." She walked to the door.

Chester moved from his place against the wall and kissed the top of her head. "Rest." His expression weary, showed signs of the resolution she had seen in Andrew.

Steven at the foot of her bed pointed to the door. "I'm right outside."

The only two left inside the small sterile room, Matthew's silhouette centered in the window. There was something more.

Sleep tugged at Jessica, eyelids heavy with exhaustion, her will drained. Footsteps, cautious, he stood beside her. His lips touched her, warmth radiated. The hospital door closed as the tears slipped over her cheeks.

CHAPTER 25

The bakery bell chimed announcing her arrival.

Sam Caldwell's head peeked out the kitchen pass through. Throwing the towel on the counter, she rushed to the front of the shop.

"Need'n a cup-a-joe, my cupboards are bare." Jessica's request muffled in the folds of Sam's shirt as she hugged her.

"You look great..." Sam held Jessica at arm's length. "Should you be driving yet, after all it's only been--"

"Doc Andrew does a sufficient job of lecturing me. All I want from you is some good conversation and a cup of coffee."

Sam flipped the "OPEN" sign to "CLOSED".

Jessica sat down.

"You doing okay?" Sam poured Jessica a cup of coffee.

Jessica nodded, viewing the town square outside the bakery window. She was thankful the twister had missed the center of town, skirting the edge, the fire station the hardest hit along with several acreages, including hers.

It had been over a month since they had sat here together. Sam had come to see her regularly in the hospital. Over the course of the visits, Jessica had shared the secrets that had turned the world she once knew upside down. The friendship had become very important to her.

"Have you spoken to Matthew?"

"What do I say?" Jessica's eyes left her cup. "How about Steven?"

"Aren't we a pair?" Sam got up, moving to the shop's coffee maker.

There was a tapping at the door.

Jessica now up, took comfort in Hannah's arms.

"Ladies, I'm late!" She grinned and winked.

All three procured their respective positions by the front window.

"Are you supposed to be tooling around on your own?" Hannah frowned.

Jessica hung her head in a weak portrayal of guilt.

"A certain doctor told you to take it easy once you got home." Hannah wagged her finger. "We were to bring you whatever you needed."

"I *needed* a Friday meeting." Jessica toasted with her coffee mug.

"Amen!" Sam clinked her cup with Jessica's.

Jessica suspected their thoughts, like hers, pondered all that had transpired.

"You knew, didn't you Hannah?"

The gray haired woman nodded.

"Nothing to hide." Jessica pointed at Sam. "She knows."

Hannah, usually boisterous, was reserved, "I didn't know as much as Chester and Andrew, but I had figured out over the years the hatred Jonas had for Joseph Cassidy had to do with more than the land."

Hannah tilted the pitcher of cream. Picking up the spoon next to her cup, she swirled the rich dark liquid until the coffee transformed to a light caramel color.

"Matthew came into the restaurant that day, late summer, hotter than Hades. That boy was so damn nervous. He walked up to Jonas, dead serious. I nearly keeled over." She blew on the caramel pool. "I didn't hear the entire conversation, just enough."

Hannah glanced at Jessica. "I'd watched you two for years. The way you picked on each other." She smiled wryly. "Even this old woman knows there's a fine line between love and hate."

The heat rose into Jessica's temples.

"I was furious with your grandfather. Cussed him up one side and down the other. Doing whatever it took to keep you two apart because of some old grudge." She shook her head. "He wouldn't budge. I threatened to stick my nose in. That's when he told me why."

Pity and sadness held for Matthew drifted onto Hannah's face. "I thought that boy was going to die." She slowly stirred her coffee again. "Then, after awhile, it changed."

She seemed to hear what ran through Jessica's head.

"Oh, he wasn't sure if or how much Jonas had told me. He didn't ask, and I didn't volunteer."

Hannah's brow pinched, her eyes imploring her to

accept. "He did it because of a promise to your grandfather. He did it because he was terrified. He did it Jess, because he loves you."

Sam squeezed Jessica's hand reassuringly.

"There's more, honey." Hannah let Jessica regain her composure. "Matthew, in true lawyer fashion, cross-examined Jonas on everything he showed him, which wasn't much. It drove your grandfather half crazy." Amusement alighted.

"They became friends and when the land deal..." She stopped, sipping her coffee. "Well, it was an opportunity to right a wrong."

Tearing it open, Hannah poured a pack of sugar into her coffee cup. "Joseph was beside himself at the thought of their friendship." Picking up the spoon, she stirred. "The devil had nothin' on that man."

A timer signaled another batch ready in the bakery's oven.

Sam scooted from the booth.

"Why couldn't he tell me?"

"Only Matthew can answer that Jess."

Wisdom had a name. Hannah Johnston.

CHAPTER 26

Jessica had missed Hannah and Sam's companionship. Although tired, the Friday morning "meeting" had definitely improved her spirits.

She sat among the papers scattered throughout the office.

Amazingly, the barn had withstood the tornado except for the roof of the office, the repairs to it almost complete. A lot of people had pitched in during her hospital stay.

She didn't hear the car and jumped at the sound of Andrew tapping on the glass of the office window. Jessica was surprised to see Chester closing the door, keeping out the winter chill.

"You promised me if I discharged you early you'd behave."

Jessica met Andrew's reprimand with a kiss to his wizened cheek as she stood.

Chester hugged her.

Andrew assessed the room. "You're not over-doing it?"

No mistaking the meaning behind his question, the

doctor was quite familiar with the papers.

"I'm cleaning files." She smiled. "For good."

Jessica didn't want either man to endure anymore. "Steven is coming out later today to help me with this."

Scratching his head, Andrew took the chair beside the desk.

Chester leaned on the edge opposite Andrew.

Jessica sat in the leather chair between the two old men.

"You've dealt with a lot lately." Andrew looked out the window of the office.

The northwest wind pushed the colored leaves and corn stalks across the fields, heralding the winter season promised.

Andrew was taking in the years, and Jessica recognized how much he missed Jonas on days like this.

"I wish he could have discovered this, Jess." The gentle soul's aged hand ran through his windblown hair then into his coat.

Jessica's chest thudded. The envelope he held matched the color of the paper the letter was written on. The letter she'd found between the paintings in the loft.

"He was coming down the loft stairs, this envelope clutched in his hand, when I arrived. The news articles, the ones you found, spread out on the desk." Chester's voice hushed, the memory, vivid.

The retired sheriff relived the last few hours of his friend's life, producing a shadow on his worn face. "I listened to what he had concluded. And although I suspected he was right, I never told him what I had."

"You see, until this envelope, it all pointed to Joseph.

The letters, the locket..." Andrew shook his head.

"Where did this come from?" Jessica motioned to the yellowed envelope lying on the desk between.

"Jonas understood he didn't have much longer. He never said it, but in the way he was desperate to get things in order, his will, the lock box, how he wanted us to handle all of this..." Doctor Andrew Harrison's voice waned.

Jessica's stomach began to feel like it had in the hospital room.

Andrew watched her.

"I'm okay Andrew, go on." Stiffness had set in challenging Jessica to be in one position too long.

"Jonas had been up in the loft working. My guess is that's where he found it among your mother's paintings." Andrew stopped, rubbing his forehead. "When he'd called me that night, something was terribly wrong." Andrew tapped the envelope. "Jonas told me he had proof of who your father was."

"I didn't know what to think and that stubborn SOB wouldn't tell me anything." The doctor's face reflected how much the call had haunted him. "Between us three old men, we had all the pieces that pointed to Maggie."

Jessica reached out to Andrew.

"The envelope was on the desk that morning." Chester Caughlin sounded tired. "He was burning a stack of papers when I left the night before. The news articles were gone so I assumed he just hadn't been able to bring himself to destroy it." Chester nodded towards the small-yellowed envelope. "I took it before it could do any more harm. But I didn't do a very good job." The sheriff paused. "The page you found, Jessica, was only part of the envelope's contents."

Fear, electric in its movement, shot through Jessica's body.

"Honey."

Jessica turned towards Andrew.

"It's the closure you're searching for."

He placed it in her open palm. She knew she should read it.

"I'm guessing he dropped the page of the letter when he was up in the loft that night. And the articles he must have knocked off the desk by accident."

Andrew concluded, "Everything happens for a reason, Jess."

The two men, quiet, measured her, taking it all in.

Andrew spoke, first to break the heavy silence, "What time are you expecting Steven?"

She glanced at the clock. It was well into the afternoon.

"He's bringing a late lunch out, should be any minute now."

Her hunger pains had subsided, curbed by what lay in her hand.

Andrew got up.

"You know, Jess, the reason behind all the secrecy was to protect the little girl we love, because her mother and father weren't here to do it." Andrew shook his head. "They were here for you more than we could have ever imagined." The door closed behind them.

Jessica caught the sun as it flashed off the gleaming fins

of Andrew's Eldorado.

***

Steven saw the dirt rising from the other side of the hill and in the spirit of gravel road etiquette, moved to the right side.

Dr. Andrew Harrison's Cadillac roared over the crest of the dirt road.

The man drives like his hair is on fire.

He raised his chin, acknowledging Steven.

Steven followed the lane up to the office. She'd been working most of the day no doubt. He reached into the back seat of the red sports car for Hannah's food.

Along with the home cooked meals, the longtime café owner served Steven a healthy portion of *what Jessica should and should not be doing while recovering,* which he had every intention of relaying. *Hell hath no fury.*

She'd packed more than the two would ever be able to eat, he hadn't argued. It would've just fired her up. *No wonder that woman had never had a husband.*

The gravel crunched under his thick-soled hiking boots. *Damn.* No matter how many places he'd been, nothing was colder than those first winter winds of Iowa. He opened the door to the office and stepped inside, shutting it as quickly as possible.

"Your lunch has arrived, Miss McCabe."

Jessica looked up from the page, patterns of pain trailed off her face.

"Should you be reading all of this stuff again?" Steven set the food on the desk then joined her on the bottom step of the loft stairs.

He instantly recognized the letter. Then he noticed...*two pages*. Steven's mind switched into journalist mode, but his instincts were cut short as Jessica began to read.

> *Dearest Peter,*
>
> *The annulment is final as of today. And now I can tell you what my heart has ached to do.*
>
> *I do not hate you. And time will help me not to hate what has always kept you just beyond.*
>
> *Others believe what they will. You must know, forever you, only you.*
>
> *So now hold dear your truest love, and I will pray for your fulfillment. I will never know you again, yet I too shall be content.*
>
> *For this God, who won your heart, has given me a gift that shall sustain me in the hours and days I will spend loving a man I can never have.*

"This proves it, Jess."

Reality flooded her eyes.

"Honey, he didn't even know you existed."

"It was a letter she never sent." She swallowed. "But it got delivered right on time."

Steven and Jessica worked side by side, boxing some

items, burning many. Steven had brought the artwork down from the loft so she could sort in the heated office. And so he could keep an eye on her.

As she dusted off each, he observed a little girl delighting in yet another buried treasure, found. A welcome sight.

"What do you think?" She pointed at the sorted stacks. "That pile will go to the school, that one to City Hall. And that group to the library."

"Sounds like a plan." Steven winked his approval.

"Steven."

Jessica sat in front of Peter's portrait, the likeness to her father, his uncle, irrefutable.

"I would like your mom to have this."

Steven's throat caught, it would mean the world to his mother. She had dealt with a great deal, like Jessica.

Conversations shared by the two women during Jessica's hospital stay had done more than anyone or anything could to help work through the history of hidden secrets.

"She'd like that, Jess."

Jessica secured the brown paper around the painting with twine.

She needed to get on with life.

"Jonas trusted Matthew, Jess, he depended on him. Don't judge him by what you *think* you know."

She stopped twisting the strings of twine around the painting in front of her and drifted out the office window. "I'm not sure where to go from here."

"Yes you are."

"And how goes it with our favorite bakery owner?" Jessica shot the question as she flipped and sorted the next stack.

"Okay, that's only fair." Steven had not said a word to Jessica about Sam. But she knew him, better sometimes than he knew himself. "I think I screwed that one up." He turned to the door lugging the container marked for burning. "The only person worse at commitment than you, Miss McCabe, is me." He walked out to the mesh enclosure of the burn pile.

CHAPTER 27

The crisp breeze filled her nostrils as she retrieved wood from the stack along the garage. Smoke curled, ascending out the chimney. It signaled the coming of one of her favorite seasons. Unlike those who dreaded the first winds that announced an Iowa winter, Sam Caldwell rejoiced in their arrival.

Reaching the house, she set the wood neatly on top of the pile that had begun to dwindle. The weather report predicted a good chance of snow by morning and she would rather haul wood now than through a foot of newly fallen snow.

Brushing her coat off, she went inside. The simmering pot of stew, put on earlier, elicited a growl. She hadn't eaten since that morning when Hannah and Jessica had stopped by. It had been good to sit with them, a conversation well overdue.

As she dipped the ladle, the doorbell rang.

A few flakes had begun to fill the air, and a dusting covered the top of his head.

"Hey Sam, I hope this isn't a bad time?"

"Not if you're hungry for some stew." She hung Matthew's coat on the hook to the left of the entry. "I've got plenty."

"Sounds good."

Matthew followed her into the kitchen.

"I was going to eat in front of the fire."

The stew's savory aroma filled the air as she ladled a heaping serving into each bowl. Placing them on saucers, Sam and Matthew headed to the front room.

The fire's heat enfolded the room, creating a cozy setting. They each placed their bowls of stew on the coffee table that stood between the furniture in front of the fireplace.

Sam handed Matthew a pillow as they sat Indian style on either side. Steam warned it would be wise to let the contents cool.

"Well, I oughta come here more often."

"It's usually not this good." She stirred her stew, blowing. "Trust me."

Matthew sat immersed in the fire.

She waited patiently. He was here for a reason.

Turning back to the steaming bowl, she watched as he picked up his spoon, poking at the vegetables and meat that floated in the thick beef broth.

"One of you has to make the first move."

"You're one to talk." Matthew's sarcastic grin hid little.

"Matthew, she needs someone." Sam stirred the beefy

broth. "And that someone is you."

"What if she can't forgive me, Sam?" Matthew stared into the fire. "What if..." he stopped as he had that day in the bakery.

Sam, up from the floor, gingerly placed another piece of wood on the burning logs. "Either way, she deserves to know, as badly as you need to get it off your conscious."

"You are a wise one, Miss Caldwell." Matthew scooped up a hearty helping of stew and gave a thumbs up.

"I can't guarantee you it'll be alright once you tell her." Sam, back in her place, leaned on the couch behind her. "But Jonas McCabe suffered with the unanswered till the day it ended up taking his life. Don't give her that same fate, Matthew."

"Taking lessons from Hannah, are we?"

"That's a backhanded compliment." She reached for the empty bowls. "I guess I'll take it. Another helping?"

"That was plenty."

"You stir the fire while I take care of this." Sam nodded to the dwindling flames. Picking up the empty bowls, she walked out to the kitchen.

"How about a drink after that stew?"

She returned with his request. "She's at home all day tomorrow. I'm taking supper out around 6:00."

"Is she taking care of herself?" Matthew accepted the cold long neck bottle without hesitation.

"No." Sam settled on the couch across from where Matthew had landed. "But for Jessica she's doing okay." She took a drink.

"Has Mr. Conrad paid you a visit lately?"

Matthew's candor irritated her.

He lifted his bottle. "You're part of the club, my friend."

Sam held her tongue. She had no argument.

They allowed the fire to mesmerize.

"Well your company has been wonderful, Miss Caldwell. Now I better hit the road before I get snowed in." He stood, and taking her empty bottle with his, carried it out to the kitchen. He entered the front foyer as Sam retrieved his coat.

"By the way, Betty said you stopped by the office yesterday while I was out." Matthew zipped his coat. "And you left behind a dozen sweet rolls. May I ask what warranted such a nice surprise?"

"Probably the same reason you were hungry for stew." Sam smirked.

Matthew got to the bottom step and stopped. "I will tell her, Sam. Promise you'll be there for her."

He walked through the snow to his truck.

Back in front of the fire, the flames entranced Sam. It was well after midnight when she went up the stairs to bed.

CHAPTER 28

The box sat empty, its contents now ashes cooling within the fireplace.

Matthew stood up from the chair that faced the hearth. A half hour later, he was showered and dressed.

He could see Sam through the window of her shop as he turned to lock the front door of his office. The tall lanky figure crossing the square generated a smile.

***

Saturday mornings were usually pretty busy. A Saturday with fresh snow on the ground always proved to be a day where you met yourself coming and going. The bell rang. Sam huffed in anticipation of the wild day ahead. "I'll be right up. Feel free to grab yourself a cup."

She pulled the trays of hot cinnamon rolls from the oven and slid the next round of baking in.

"Samantha Caldwell, you are amazing."

Sam didn't react at first. Then, steeling herself she drew on the tenacious will she had been born with.

Steven stood in the doorway to the kitchen, appearing to seek permission to come in. Not something she expected.

"Well you must really need a cup of coffee bad." She continued at the counter adding ingredients.

"Sam."

She kept moving, pretending not to detect his uneasiness. Her defenses up, Sam clicked into survival mode and "the cadence". *I can't do this. I won't do this.* She had seen the way he looked at Jessica, regardless of what had been discovered.

"Samantha." He was now behind her. "Please."

Sam placed the measuring cup on the counter. Facing out the bright, frost covered window, she mustered every ounce of strength she could gather.

"I cannot do this, Steven," her delivery, clear and direct, as she had rehearsed. "I am not her."

Steven's silent affirmation was shattering. Shaking, she fumbled for the measuring cup.

"I have been places in my life that take your breath away."

Close behind her, he hadn't moved. His voice, deep, soft, vibrated in her chest.

"I always believed that somewhere in those distant worlds I would find--"

The egg splattered at Sam's feet. Her effort to be aloof, unfazed by his proximity, gone.

He turned her to him.

"Samantha Caldwell." He cupped her chin.

She backed away. "You think this is what you want,

Steven, but..." Her eyes came upon the wooden recipe box. She couldn't breathe.

He held it out to her.

Slowly opening the lid Sam found herself taken in by a beautiful recipe card and the handwriting upon it.

I have searched all my life for you
And you were here all along
Next to my heart, my soul
Calling my name

You are the answer to the prayer
I whisper alone at night
When no one else can hear
I love you, Samantha Caldwell

Tears blessed the lid. "So is this a tribal ritual from some far off country you've been to?"

"Well as a matter-of-fact, it is sacred tradition in the tribe of Conrad, that when a man loves a woman he must express his undying allegiance by giving her a recipe box." He stepped closer.

The quaking emerged. Nothing could stop it.

"Look at me, Samantha."

Sam raised her gaze and fell into the eyes of Steven Conrad.

"Please accept this box and this man before you, fool that he has been."

He began to kiss her and Sam let herself go where her

heart had always been.

***

The light on in the office, Matthew knocked on the door then opened it. "Jess?"

He heard her footsteps above his head. Jessica ducked through the stairwell moving slower than usual. She was still sore.

"Are you supposed to be up there?"

"Just a few things left to put away."

Matthew followed her up the stairs into the large room. The autumn air revealed his breath.

"You're going to town up here." Matthew noted the neatly organized storage room.

"Jonas was a packrat." She glanced over her shoulder. "Unfortunately his granddaughter tends to be one too." She went back to sorting.

The pile of letters and the box were impossible to miss.

He'd run it over and over in his mind. How he would tell her. It did little to help now.

"I had gone to Jonas to share with him I was madly in love with his granddaughter."

Outside the loft window, the snow had begun to fall again.

"I was going to propose to you." Matthew's throat tightened. "I'll never forget his face...an agony, almost physical...

"He refused to give me a reason at first. I couldn't comprehend the hate and jealousy he harbored for my father. A level that wouldn't even allow his granddaughter's happiness. I decided with or without his blessing..." His eyes went to her frozen figure.

"Later that afternoon I stepped into his office door to confront him, fully prepared for the argument he would give me. There was none. He was sitting at his desk, the box and the letters from my father in front of him. He told me to read them."

Jessica sank to the floor amid the letters, curling her knees up to her chest. He wanted to go to her but continued.

"He was scared to death Jess, scared that I would tell you, that my father would claim you. Terrified at what it would do to you." Matthew ran his hand through his hair.

"I had so many questions... And we argued." Matthew had started that day to become acquainted with and more importantly appreciate the warm-hearted soul, Jonas McCabe. Until then he had only known the man through his father's twisted, distorted view.

"Why would you want me to live with such a lie?"

It was taking every bit of strength in her sore, tired body to keep it together. Matthew said a silent prayer, *"God, help her to see."*

"I would be in the truck, dialing the phone, writing a letter..." Matthew staggered under the weight of the memory, its consequence. "Then I'd see the agony in Jonas' face.

"I don't understand..."

"Jess." Matthew crossed the loft to her and knelt down. Fatigue gripped her, but she must hear why it had all gone so far.

"Chester wasn't the only one to talk to your grandfather

the night before he died."

The shock washed across her.

Dear God, give me the words.

"Jonas had always been adamant under what circumstances and how you would be told. He knew the day would come. Then a month before he died something changed. Something was wrong. Now, thinking back, it must've been when he first found the envelope in the loft that contained the letter.

"He called that night saying over and over again how he had made a terrible mistake." Matthew paused. "He begged me not to come out.

"When I got here he was sitting in the chair, staring out the window. All the articles were spread out on the desk...and the letter..." Matthew's voice faltered.

Puffs of white hovered in the air as she cried. Gently, Matthew wiped Jessica's cold pink cheeks.

"I decided at that moment it had consumed one life and it would not consume another. We decided to burn them.

"Then out of the blue he asked me to go. He wanted to destroy them, in the same fashion he had dealt with most of this the last 30 years, alone. I did as he asked. That's when he called Chester."

Jessica's shoulders began to rise and fall.

"Until then it all led to the conclusion that Joseph was our father. The letters, the broken locket and the words your mother spoke the night she died." His arms ached to hold her.

"Jonas' discovery and your mother's supposed link to Peter's death, it changed everything, except for one."

Her visible anguish intensified.

"I had kept Jonas's secret as promised. And now that there was a chance, it was worse than he had imagined. I was determined to protect you from the pain he lived and died with.

"Until my mother saw that locket and all it held about your mother's innocence..." He looked into her tear-filled eyes. "We were willing to do anything to keep you from the truth that haunted Jonas."

Matthew listened as the wind howled and watched as the snow blew. "I died when I lost you," his husky voice trembled, "and I will understand if this is more than you can ever forgive."

Her silence triggered a cold fear once again.

He stood up, unsure if his legs could carry him away.

Turning the key in the ignition, he looked out the windshield of his truck. The sight of her trudging through the drifts of snow caused the fog of emotion to run.

The two solitary figures became one as the Iowa snow swirled around them.

EPILOGUE

The early morning sun cascaded through the stained glass windows of St. John's Catholic Church and bathed the altar in a rainbow of light.

He wiggled and his father placed the pacifier between the beautiful pink lips.

They followed the priest to the baptismal font left of the altar.

"Life is a precious gift. And today we are rejoicing in the baptism of a new life in God's church." Dipping the silver baptismal shell into the basin of the marble font, Father Patrick poured the holy water onto the chubby cheeked, dark haired bundle wrapped in white.

Hannah Johnston reached for the handkerchief she always had tucked up her sleeve.

"Jonas, I baptize you in the name of the Father and of the Son and of the Holy Spirit. Amen."

Matthew turned towards the parish as they applauded their newest member.

Jonas Matthew Cassidy let out a scream easily heard above the clapping.

"Just like his grandfather." Chester Caughlin nudged Dr. Andrew Harrison.

The two godfathers chuckled.

The smiles that surrounded the baptismal font confirmed. He had been christened with the right name.

Jessica looked at the men in her life and then at the precious little boy nestled in her arms, God's reminder that love, no matter how lost, will find its way home.

Acknowledgments

True writers know that writing is not something they feel required to do, or to make a living they must do, it is quite frankly like breathing. Some can breathe often and fluently, some short breaths, some a long exhale and for many of us it is the patient steady breathing surrounding life.

Many have helped me breathe through this novel and for that, I am so very grateful.

First and foremost my husband Kent who has championed me through it all. God could not have blessed me more.

Our children who everyday amaze me in the little things that are so very big! You are proof of love in this world!

God's first gift to me were parents who whether knowingly or not instilled in us that we could do anything. It was just a matter of how were we going to get it done. That stubbornness, handed down generation to generation is worth its weight in gold.

To Diane Bahrenfuss who was the first outside the "circle of trust" to read my novel and graced me with her wisdom and insight. Thank you.

Finally, to those who along the way encouraged and supported in ways you may not even realize.

Faith, Always

About the Author

Milissa R. Bailey, along with her husband, own a marketing firm located in Iowa.

Her debut novel draws upon her rich knowledge of the Midwest where she was born, raised and continues to live with her husband, and three children.

She is currently at work on the second book in the Gracier series. Visit her website www.milissarbailey.com